苦練出來的語言最美

　　全世界都知道，傳統英語教學最大的缺點，就是學了不會說。多少人從小學到大學，努力學英文，學了幾十年，還是不會開口說。少數會說幾句英語的人，說起來沒有信心，結結巴巴，因為不知道自己說的對還是錯，大多不敢張開嘴巴，有信心地大聲說。

　　小孩子記憶力強，背東西背得快，但是忘得也快。「小學生英語演講」有固定格式，孩子可以一篇接一篇地背下去。只要將「小學生英語演講」背完，就能夠連續講英文 30 分鐘以上，腦筋裡面就儲存了 540 個句子，可以做無限多的排列組合，每個句子背熟後，就會變成一個句型，可以舉一反三。

　　背單字不如背句子，背了單字不見得會用，背了句子馬上就可以用。背一個句子會忘，背三個句子也會忘，連續背九個句子，串連在一起，就不容易忘記。「一口氣英語」系列，每一回九句，每一本十二回，共 108 句，孩子們背完之後，就可以和外國人做簡單的交談。

　　學語言最大的困難是，學了會忘記，學了等於白學。有了「一口氣英語」後，只要將每一本「一口氣英語」，背到一分鐘之內，就終生不會忘記。背了十本，就有 1080 句，從小開始背，日積月累下來，不得了。

會用英語演講，能增加領袖氣質

　　「小學生英語演講」內容全部取材自美國口語的精華，可利用演講中的內容，和外國人深談，也可寫出動人的文章。一般美國人寫文章會錯，但你用「小學生英語演講」中的句子，組合成文章，就非常精彩了。

　　小孩子從小養成背英語演講的習慣，有了目標，腦筋不會亂想，**一篇接一篇地背下去，很有成就感。**演講中的內容，無形中也陶冶了身心。從小就會上台用英語演講，長大就不得了，可以成為國際級的領袖人物。

　　很多父母為了讓小孩學英文，把小孩送到國外去，想不到，一些小留學生回國後，說起英文來，像是含在嘴巴裡一樣，說得模模糊糊，畏畏縮縮。可能是因為他們從小在國外，和外國小孩在一起，總怕講錯話，養成嘴巴張不開的習慣。更糟糕的是，受到外國文化的影響，不中不西，一不小心，就變成邊緣人。

　　但是，如果背了「小學生英語演講」，就不一樣了。「小學生英語演講」中的每個句子，都是經過精挑細選，你說的每一句話，都是苦練過的，說起來自然有信心，自然會張開嘴巴，清清楚楚，一句一句地大聲說出來。能夠站在台上慷慨激昂地發表演說，就具有成為領袖或大人物的特質。

劉毅

目錄CONTENTS

1. Self-Introduction

Hello, my name is Donald.
I am a new student at this school.
It is my pleasure to be here.

This is an exciting time.
There are many new faces.
There will be many new names
　　to learn.

I hope to meet all of you.
I hope to be your friend.
Let me tell you about myself.

self〔sɛlf〕
introduction〔͵ɪntrə'dʌkʃən〕
pleasure〔'plɛʒɚ〕　　　　exciting〔ɪk'saɪtɪŋ〕
face〔fes〕　　　　　　　learn〔lɝn〕
hope〔hop〕　　　　　　　meet〔mit〕
friend〔frɛnd〕　　　　　tell〔tɛl〕

***I like reading and playing violin*.**
I speak three languages.
I would like to speak good English
    as well.

I come from a small family.
I don't have any siblings.
Therefore, I'm very close to my parents.

I have big plans for the future.
I would like to study medicine.
I want to be a doctor.

read〔rid〕   violin〔ˌvaɪəˈlɪn〕
play violin   speak〔spik〕
language〔ˈlæŋgwɪdʒ〕   ***would like to***
as well   ***come from***
family〔ˈfæməlɪ〕   ***small family***
siblings〔ˈsɪblɪŋz〕   therefore〔ˈðɛrˌfor〕
be close to   parents〔ˈpɛrənts〕
plan〔plæn〕   future〔ˈfjutʃɚ〕
study〔ˈstʌdɪ〕   medicine〔ˈmɛdəsn̩〕
doctor〔ˈdɑktɚ〕

1

Of course, *I am here to learn*.

But I also want to make friends.

Maybe we can have fun at the same time.

Here's what you can expect from me.

I am very polite and respectful.

I am always willing to help.

The next few years will be interesting.

We will share many experiences.

I wish the best for each and every one
   of you.

of course	also ('ɔlso)
make friends	maybe ('mebɪ)
have fun	*at the same time*
expect (ɪk'spɛkt)	polite (pə'laɪt)
respectful (rɪ'spɛktfəl)	always ('ɔlwez)
willing ('wɪlɪŋ)	next (nɛkst)
few (fju)	interesting ('ɪntrɪstɪŋ)
share (ʃɛr)	experience (ɪk'spɪrɪəns)
wish the best for	*each and every one*

1. *Self-Introduction*

🔵 演講解說

Hello, my name is Donald.	哈囉，我的名字是唐納德。
I am a new student at this school.	我是這間學校的新生。
It is my pleasure to be here.	我很榮幸能來到這裡。
This is an exciting time.	這是個令人興奮的時刻。
There are many new faces.	有很多新面孔。
There will be many new names to learn.	未來要記得很多人的名字。
I hope to meet all of you.	我希望可以認識大家。
I hope to be your friend.	我希望成為你們的朋友。
Let me tell you about myself.	讓我告訴你們關於我的事。

**

self〔sɛlf〕*n.* 自己；本身
introduction〔ˌɪntrə'dʌkʃən〕*n.* 介紹
pleasure〔'plɛdʒɚ〕*n.* 愉快；榮幸
exciting〔ɪk'saɪtɪŋ〕*adj.* 令人興奮的
face〔fes〕*n.* 臉；面孔　　learn〔lɛn〕*v.* 學習；得知；記得
hope〔hop〕*v.* 希望　　meet〔mit〕*v.* 遇見；認識
friend〔frɛnd〕*n.* 朋友　　tell〔tɛl〕*v.* 告訴

1

I like reading and playing violin.	我喜歡閱讀和拉小提琴。
I speak three languages.	我會講三種語言。
I would like to speak good English as well.	我也想要說流利的英文。
I come from a small family.	我來自一個小家庭。
I don't have any siblings.	我沒有任何兄弟姊妹。
Therefore, I'm very close to my parents.	因此，我和父母很親近。
I have big plans for the future.	我未來有遠大的計畫。
I would like to study medicine.	我想要讀醫科。
I want to be a doctor.	我想要成為醫生。

** ——————————————

read〔rid〕*v.* 閱讀　　violin〔͵vaɪə'lɪn〕*n.* 小提琴

play violin 彈小提琴（ = *play the violin* ）

speak〔spik〕*v.* 說（語言）　　language〔'læŋgwɪdʒ〕*n.* 語言

would like to V. 想要　　***as well*** 也（ = *too* ）

come from 來自於　　family〔'fæməlɪ〕*n.* 家庭

small family 小家庭　　siblings〔'sɪblɪŋz〕*n. pl.* 兄弟姊妹

therefore〔'ðɛr͵for〕*adv.* 因此　　***be close to*** 和…親近

parents〔'pɛrənts〕*n. pl.* 父母　　plan〔plæn〕*n.* 計畫

future〔'fjutʃə〕*n.* 未來　　study〔'stʌdɪ〕*v.* 研讀

medicine〔'mɛdəsn̩〕*n.* 醫學　　doctor〔'dɑktə〕*n.* 醫生

Of course, *I am here to learn*.   當然，我是來這裡學習的。
But I also want to make friends.   但我也想要交朋友。
Maybe we can have fun at the   或許我們可以同時也玩得
    same time.   開心。

Here's what you can expect   你們可以預期我是個怎麼
    from me.   樣的人。
I am very polite and respectful.   我很有禮貌並尊重他人。
I am always willing to help.   我總是願意伸出援手。

The next few years will be   接下來的幾年將會很有趣。
    interesting.
We will share many experiences.   我們將共享很多經驗。
I wish the best for each and   祝你們每一個人都一切順
    every one of you.   利。

**

of course 當然　　also (ˋɔlso) *adv.* 也
make friends 交朋友　　maybe (ˋmebɪ) *adv.* 或許；可能
have fun 玩得愉快 (= *have a good time*)
at the same time 同時　　expect (ɪkˋspɛkt) *v.* 期待；預期
polite (pəˋlaɪt) *adj.* 有禮貌的
respectful (rɪˋspɛktfəl) *adj.* 尊敬他人的；恭敬的
always (ˋɔlwez) *adv.* 總是　　willing (ˋwɪlɪŋ) *adj.* 願意的
next (nɛkst) *adj.* 接下來的　　few (fju) *adj.* 幾個；一些
interesting (ˋɪntrɪstɪŋ) *adj.* 有趣的　　share (ʃɛr) *v.* 分享；共有
experience (ɪkˋspɪrɪəns) *n.* 經驗　　*wish the best for* 祝…一切順利
each and every 每一~ (= *every*)；所有的

背景說明

　　第一天上學，老師常常會要求每位同學一一自我介紹，好讓同學認識彼此。本篇演講稿，是告訴你如何簡單明瞭地表達自己，好讓同學對你有初步的了解，並想和你交朋友。

1. *I am a new student at this school.*

　　這句話的意思是「我是這間學校的新生。」來到新學校，在介紹自己之前，常常會說到這句話，也可以說成：

This is my first day at this school.
（今天是我在這間學校的第一天。）

I'm new around here.
（我是新來的。）

【*around here*　在這附近】

2. *Let me tell you about myself.*

　　這句話的意思是「讓我告訴你們關於我的事。」可以用來作為自我介紹的開頭，讓大家知道你要開始講關於你自己的事情，也可以說成：

Allow me to introduce myself.
（讓我介紹我自己。）

Would you like to hear a little something about me?（你想要聽一些關於我的事情嗎？）

1

allow〔ə'laʊ〕*v.* 允許　　introduce〔͵ɪntrə'djus〕*v.* 介紹
would like to V. 想要　　hear〔hɪr〕*v.* 聽

3. *I like reading and playing violin*.

read〔rid〕*v.* 閱讀
play〔ple〕*v.* 彈奏（樂器）
violin〔͵vaɪə'lɪn〕*n.* 小提琴

　　這句話的意思是「我喜歡閱讀和拉小提琴。」like
（喜歡）後面可以接 to V.或 V-ing，*所以後面的* read
和 play *寫成* reading *和* playing。另外，通常表示
「彈奏樂器」時，會用「play the + 樂器」，如：play
the guitar（彈吉他）、play the piano（彈鋼琴），但
美國人現在常把 the 省略了，英國人則還是保持「the +
樂器」的型態。【詳見「Oxford Guide to Grammar」p. 393】

guitar〔gɪ'tɑr〕*n.* 吉他　　piano〔pɪ'æno〕*n.* 鋼琴

4. *I come from a small family*.

come from 來自　　*small family* 小家庭

　　這句話的意思是「我來自一個小家庭。」small
family 就是「小家庭」，定義是「一個家庭由一對夫
妻或一對夫妻加上其未婚子女所組成」。現代的都市
家庭大多是如此，也可說成：nuclear family，字面
上是「核心家庭」，也就是指「小規模的家庭」。

nuclear〔'nuklɪə〕*adj.* 核子的
nuclear family 核心家庭；小家庭

這句話也可以說成：

My family is quite small. (我的家庭很小。)
I was raised in a small but loving family.
(我生長在一個規模很小的但卻充滿愛的家庭。)

quite〔kwaɪt〕*adv.* 相當　　raise〔rez〕*v.* 撫養
loving〔'lʌvɪŋ〕*adj.* 充滿愛的

　　相反地，如果是好幾代同堂的家庭，英文說成
big family (大家庭) 或是 extended family，字
面上是「擴大的家庭」，指的是「大規模的家庭」。

extended〔ɪk'stɛndɪd〕*adj.* 擴大的
extended family 大家庭

5. ***Therefore, I'm very close to my parents.***

therefore〔'ðɛr,for〕*adv.* 因此；所以
close〔klos〕*adj.* 親近的　　***be close to*** 和…親近
parents〔'pɛrənts〕*n. pl.* 父母

　　這句話的意思是「因此，
我和父母很親近。」close 原
本是「接近的；靠近的」，be
close to 意思是「接近…的；

靠近…的」，例如：My workplace ***is close to*** the
sea. (我的工作地點靠近海。) 而 be close to 可引申
為「和…親近」，例如：He wants to ***be close to*** you.
(他想要親近你。)

【workplace〔'wɝk,ples〕*n.* 工作場所】

這句話也可說成：

Thus, my parents and I have a close
relationship.
（因此，我父母和我的關係很親密。）

Indeed, my parents are like
good friends.
（的確，我的父母就像好朋友一樣。）

relationship〔rɪ'leʃənˌʃɪp〕n. 關係
indeed〔ɪn'did〕adv. 的確

6. ***Maybe we can have fun at the same time.***

maybe〔'mebɪ〕adv. 或許；可能

have fun 玩得愉快　　***at the same time*** 同時

這句話的意思是「或許我們可以同時也玩得開心。」
去學校既可以學習新知，也可以交朋友，當然，最重
要的是，和朋友打成一片。這句話也可以說成：

It's possible to do both!（兩者都可能做得到！）

Perhaps we can enjoy the process of getting
to know each other.
（或許我們可以享受認識彼此的過程。）

possible〔'pɑsəbḷ〕adj. 可能的
perhaps〔pɚ'hæps〕adv. 或許；可能
enjoy〔ɪn'dʒɔɪ〕n. 享受
process〔'prɑsɛs〕n. 過程
get to V. 能夠
know〔no〕v. 知道；認識

7. ***Here's what you can expect from me***.

expect〔ɪk'spɛkt〕*v.* 期待；預期

1

　　這句話的意思是「你可以預期我是個怎麼樣的人。」
what 是複合關係代名詞，意思是「…的事物」，引導
名詞子句，例如：

What I say is true. (= *The thing that I say is true.*)
（我說的是真的。）

He always does what he believes is right.
(= *He always does the thing that he believes
　　is right.*)
（他總是做他認為對的事。）

true〔tru〕*adj.* 真的　　believe〔bə'liv〕*v.* 相信；認為

這句話也可以說成：

Here's what you need to know about me.
（這是你必須知道的關於我的事。）

This is the type of person I am.
（我就是這類型的人。）

【*need to V*. 需要】

8. ***I am very polite and respectful***.

polite〔pə'laɪt〕*adj.* 有禮貌的
respectful〔rɪ'spɛktfəl〕*adj.* 尊敬他人的；恭敬的

　　這句話的意思是「我很有禮貌並尊重他人。」禮貌
和尊敬可說是交朋友必要的條件。

關於禮貌，有以下的諺語：

Politeness costs nothing and gains everything.
（禮貌不費分文，卻能贏得一切。）

Courtesy on one side only lasts not long.
（一方有禮禮不長；禮尚需往來。）

politeness〔pə'laɪtnɪs〕*n.* 禮貌
cost〔kɔst〕*v.* 花費　　gain〔gen〕*v.* 獲得
courtesy〔'kɝtəsɪ〕*n.* 禮貌
side〔saɪd〕*n.* 一方　　last〔læst〕*v.* 持續

9. ***I wish the best for each and every one of you.***
wish the best for 祝…一切順利
each and every 每一

這句話的意思是「祝你們每一個人都一切順利。」
wish the best for *sb.* 也可說成 wish *sb.* (all) the
best。例如：I ***wish you all the best.*** （我祝你一切
順利。）each and every 是強調的説法，就是 each
或是 every 的意思。

這句話也可以説成：

I wish nothing but the best for all of you.
（我祝你們一切順利。）

I hope all your dreams come true.
（我希望你們心想事成。）

nothing but 只（= *only*）　　hope〔hop〕*v.* 希望
dream〔drim〕*n.* 夢想　　***come true*** 成真；實現

● 作文範例

Self-Introduction

1

Good morning, teachers and students.
This is an exciting time, **and** it is truly my
pleasure to be here. There are so many new
faces and names to learn. I hope to get to
know all of you.

Let me tell you a little about myself.
I come from a small family **and** I don't have
any siblings. I'm close to my parents, **but**
I **also** love spending time with friends.

I like reading and playing violin. I'm
also interested in languages. I speak Chinese,
Japanese, and French. I would like to speak
good English as well. It's a great way to meet
people.

● 中文翻譯

自我介紹

早安，各位老師，各位同學。這真是個令人興奮的時刻，有很多新的面孔和名字要記得。我希望可以認識你們全部的人。

讓我告訴你們一些關於我的事。我來自一個小家庭，我沒有任何兄弟姊妹。我和父母親非常親近，但我也喜歡和朋友在一起。

我喜歡閱讀和拉小提琴，我也對語言有興趣，我會講中文、日文和法文，我想也要說一口流利的英文，這是個認識朋友很好的方法。

2. My Parents

My parents play a big part in my life.
They have molded my character.
They have been my role models.

2

My parents have good moral character.
They don't smoke, drink, or gamble.
They are patient and good listeners.

My parents demonstrate good virtue in
　their actions.
They teach me to have respect.
They teach me to be kind to others.

---

parents〔'pɛrənts〕
mold〔mold〕
role model
smoke〔smok〕
gamble〔'gæmbḷ〕
listener〔'lɪsnɚ〕
virtue〔'vɝtʃʊ〕
teach〔titʃ〕
kind〔kaɪnd〕

play a…part
character〔'kærɪktɚ〕
moral〔'mɔrəl〕
drink〔drɪŋk〕
patient〔'peʃənt〕
demonstrate〔'dɛmən,stret〕
action〔'ækʃən〕
respect〔rɪ'spɛkt〕
others〔'ʌðɚz〕

My parents have raised three children.
All of us are well-adjusted.
Their influence is the reason.

My parents believe in strong communication.
They take time to listen to us.
They understand our problems.

One time, my sister failed a test.
My parents did not scold or judge her.
They simply encouraged her to try harder.

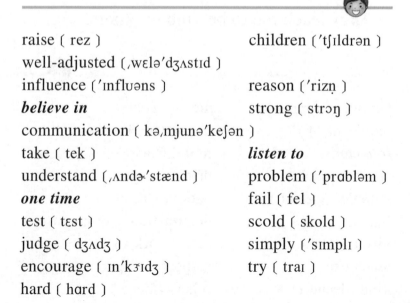

raise〔rez〕   children〔'tʃɪldrən〕
well-adjusted〔ˌwɛlə'dʒʌstɪd〕
influence〔'ɪnfluəns〕   reason〔'rizn̩〕
believe in   strong〔strɔŋ〕
communication〔kə,mjunə'keʃən〕
take〔tek〕   *listen to*
understand〔ˌʌndɚ'stænd〕   problem〔'prɑbləm〕
one time   fail〔fel〕
test〔tɛst〕   scold〔skold〕
judge〔dʒʌdʒ〕   simply〔'sɪmplɪ〕
encourage〔ɪn'kɝɪdʒ〕   try〔traɪ〕
hard〔hɑrd〕

Having patience is important for a parent.
My parents always go the extra mile.
Their patience has no limit.

Being a parent is a tough job.
It comes with a lot of responsibility.
Sacrifices must be made.

In modern times, parenting is complicated.
It takes good character to raise good kids.
That's why my parents make me proud to
    be their child.

2

---

patience ('peʃəns)
important (ɪm'portn̩t)   always ('ɔlwez)
extra ('ɛkstrə)   mile (maɪl)
go the extra mile
tough (tʌf)   job (dʒɑb)
come with   ***a lot of***
responsibility (rɪˌspɑnsə'bɪlətɪ)
sacrifice ('sækrəˌfaɪs)   modern ('mɑdə·n)
times (taɪmz)   parenting ('pɛrəntɪŋ)
complicated ('kɑmpləˌketɪd)
take (tek)   kid (kɪd)
proud (praʊd)   child (tʃaɪld)

2. *My Parents*

● 演講解說

My parents play a big part in my life.	我父母在我的人生中扮演重大的角色。
They have molded my character.	他們塑造我的人格。
They have been my role models.	他們是我的楷模。
My parents have good moral character.	我的父母有良好的品德。
They don't smoke, drink, or gamble.	他們不抽煙、喝酒或賭博。
They are patient and good listeners.	他們很有耐心，是很好的聆聽者。
My parents demonstrate good virtue in their actions.	我的父母在行為方面表現出良好的美德。
They teach me to have respect.	他們教我要尊重他人。
They teach me to be kind to others.	他們教我要善待他人。

＊＊ ─────────────

parents〔'pɛrənts〕*n. pl.* 父母   *play a…part* 扮演…的角色
big〔bɪg〕*adj.* 大的；重要的   mold〔mold〕*v.* 塑造
character〔'kærɪktɚ〕*n.* 人格；品行   *role model* 楷模
moral〔'mɔrəl〕*adj.* 道德的   smoke〔smok〕*v.* 抽煙
drink〔drɪŋk〕*v.* 喝酒   gamble〔'gæmbḷ〕*v.* 賭博
patient〔'peʃənt〕*adj.* 有耐心的   listener〔'lɪsn̩ɚ〕*n.* 聆聽者
demonstrate〔'dɛmən,stret〕*v.* 表現   virtue〔'vɜtʃu〕*n.* 美德
action〔'ækʃən〕*n.* 行動；行為   teach〔titʃ〕*v.* 教導
respect〔rɪ'spɛkt〕*n.* 尊敬；尊重
kind〔kaɪnd〕*adj.* 仁慈的；親切的   others〔'ʌðɚz〕*n. pl.* 別人

My parents have raised three children.	我的父母撫養了三個小孩。
All of us are well-adjusted.	我們全都適應良好。
Their influence is the reason.	這是因為他們的影響。
My parents believe in strong communication.	我父母相信良好溝通的力量。
They take time to listen to us.	他們花時間聽我們講話。
They understand our problems.	他們了解我們的問題。
One time, my sister failed a test.	有一次,我妹妹考試不及格。
My parents did not scold or judge her.	我爸媽並沒有責罵或批評她。
They simply encouraged her to try harder.	他們只是鼓勵她要更努力。

**　**

** ───────────────

raise〔rez〕v. 養育　　children〔ˋtʃɪldrən〕n. pl. 兒童(child 的複數)
well-adjusted〔ˋwɛləˌdʒʌstɪd〕adj. 適應良好的;性格健全的
influence〔ˋɪnfluəns〕n. 影響　　reason〔ˋrizṇ〕n. 原因
believe in 相信…的效用　　strong〔strɔŋ〕adj. 強烈的;有力的
communication〔kəˌmjunəˋkeʃən〕n. 溝通　　take〔tek〕v. 花費
listen to 聆聽　　understand〔ˌʌndəˋstænd〕v. 了解
problem〔ˋprɑbləm〕n. 問題　　***one time*** 有一次
fail〔fel〕v. (考試)不及格　　test〔tɛst〕n. 考試;測驗
scold〔skold〕v. 責罵　　judge〔dʒʌdʒ〕v. 批評;指責
simply〔ˋsɪmplɪ〕adv. 只(= only)
encourage〔ɪnˋkɝɪdʒ〕v. 鼓勵　　try〔traɪ〕v. 嘗試
hard〔hɑrd〕adv. 努力地(比較級 harder)

***Having patience is important for a parent*.**

有耐心對父母來說是很重要的。

My parents always go the extra mile.

我的父母總是付出更多。

Their patience has no limit.

他們的耐心沒有極限。

Being a parent is a tough job.

當一個父母是很困難的。

It comes with a lot of responsibility.

這伴隨著很多責任。

Sacrifices must be made.

犧牲是必要的。

In modern times, parenting is complicated.

在現代,養育子女是很複雜的。

It takes good character to raise good kids.

需要有好的品德才能養育出好的小孩。

That's why my parents make me proud to be their child.

那就是為什麼我會覺得當我父母的小孩很自豪。

** ─────────────

patience〔'peʃəns〕n. 耐心　　important〔ɪm'pɔrtṇt〕adj. 重要的
extra〔'ɛkstrə〕adj. 額外的　　mile〔maɪl〕n. 英里
go the extra mile 付出更多　　limit〔'lɪmɪt〕n. 限制;極限
tough〔tʌf〕adj. 困難的　　job〔dʒab〕n. 工作　　**come with** 伴隨
a lot of 很多的　　responsibility〔rɪ,spansə'bɪlətɪ〕n. 責任
sacrifice〔'sækrə,faɪs〕n. 犧牲　　modern〔'madən〕adj. 現代的
times〔taɪmz〕n. pl. 時代
parenting〔'pɛəntɪŋ〕n. 子女的養育
complicated〔'kamplə,ketɪd〕adj. 複雜的　　take〔tek〕v. 需要
kid〔kɪd〕n. 小孩　　proud〔praud〕adj. 驕傲的;自豪的
child〔tʃaɪld〕n. 小孩

背景說明

　　話說「教育始於家庭」(Education begins at home.)，可見家庭教育的重要性。從小開始，父母便對孩子的教育佔有舉足輕重的地位，因此，本篇演講稿，要教你如何表達父母對你的教育及影響。

2

1. **_My parents play a big part in my life_**.

parents〔ˈpɛrənts〕_n. pl._ 父母　　play〔ple〕_v._ 扮演
big〔bɪg〕_adj._ 大的；重要的　　part〔pɑrt〕_n._ 角色

　　這句話的意思是「我父母在我的人生中扮演重要的角色。」這裡的 play 是「扮演（角色）」的意思，play a~part 字面是「扮演一個~部分」，引申為「扮演一個~角色」，也可以寫成 play a role，例如：Communication skills **_play a big role in_** interpersonal relationships.
（溝通技巧在人際關係上扮演重要的角色。）

role〔rol〕_n._ 角色
communication〔kə͵mjunəˈkeʃən〕_n._ 溝通
skill〔skɪl〕_n._ 技巧
interpersonal〔͵ɪntɚˈpɝsn̩l〕_adj._ 人際的
relationship〔rɪˈleʃən͵ʃɪp〕_n._ 關係

這句話也可以說成：

　　My parents have a major impact on my life.
　　（我父母對我的人生有重大的影響。）

2

My life is directly influenced by my parents.
（我父母對我的人生有直接的影響。）

major〔'medʒɚ〕*adj.* 主要的；重大的
impact〔'ɪmpækt〕*n.* 影響
have an impact on 對⋯有影響
directly〔dǝ'rɛktlɪ〕*adv.* 直接地
influence〔'ɪnfluǝns〕*v.* 影響

2. ***They have molded my character.***
mold〔mold〕*v.* 塑造
character〔'kærɪktɚ〕*n.* 人格；品行

　　　這句話的意思是「他們塑造我的人格。」mold 當
名詞時作「模型」解，動詞引申為「塑造」。character
是不要和characteristic（特色）搞混了。
例如：Some animals possess the ***characteristics***
of man.（有些動物有人類的特性。）

characteristic〔ˌkærɪktǝ'rɪstɪk〕*n.* 特色；特性
animal〔'ænǝml̩〕*n.* 動物　　possess〔pǝ'zɛs〕*v.* 擁有
man〔mæn〕*n.* 人類（＝ *mankind*）

這句話也可以說成：

They have made me what I am today.
（他們造就我今天的樣子。）

My character is a result of what they have
　taught me.（我的人格是他們教導的結果。）

【***what*** *one* ***is*** 某人的樣子　　result〔rɪ'zʌlt〕*n.* 結果】

3. *My parents demonstrate good virtue in their actions*.

demonstrate〔'dɛmən,stret〕*v.* 表現；示範

virtue〔'vɝtʃʊ〕*n.* 美德　　action〔'ækʃən〕*n.* 行動；行為

這句話的意思是「我父母在行為方面展現出良好的美德。」俗話説：「身教重於言教。」父母自己以身作則，表現美德，便是最好的教育：

2

Example is better than precept.

（身教重於言教。）

Practice what you preach.

（言行一致；説到做到。）

example〔ɪg'zæmpḷ〕*n.* 例子；榜樣
precept〔'prisɛpt〕*n.* 教訓；告誡
practice〔'præktɪs〕*v.* 實踐
preach〔pritʃ〕*v.* 倡導；訓誡

這句話也可以説成：

My parents value good behavior over words.

（我的父母認為良好的行為比言語重要。）

My parents show integrity by how they treat
　　others.（我的父母藉由待人處事來展現正直。）

value〔'væljʊ〕*v.* 重視
value A *over* B　認為 A 比 B 重要
behavior〔bɪ'hevjɚ〕*n.* 行為
words〔wɝds〕*n. pl.* 言語；話　　show〔ʃo〕*v.* 表現
integrity〔ɪn'tɛgrətɪ〕*n.* 正直　　teat〔trit〕*v.* 對待

4. ***All of us are well-adjusted.***

well-adjusted〔'wɛlə,dʒʌstɪd〕*adj.* 適應環境的；
適應良好的

　　　這句話的意思是「我們全都適應良好。」adjust
〔ə'dʒʌst〕*v.* 適應，和介系詞 to 連用，以 adjust to
或 adjust *oneself* to 的型態出現。例如：

He soon ***adjusted to*** army life.
（他很快就適應了軍隊生活。）

You must ***adjust yourself to*** new conditions.
（你必須讓自己適應新的環境。）

army〔'ɑrmɪ〕*adj.* 軍隊的
conditions〔kən'dɪʃənz〕*n. pl.* 環境；情況

能夠適應社會，表示能了解並遵守社會上的總總禮俗、
待人接物等，這句話也可以說成：

We are all well-balanced and stable citizens.
（我們都是健全而安穩的公民。）

We all know right from wrong.
（我們都分辨是非。）

Each of us has common sense.
（我們每個人都有常識。）

well-balanced〔'wɛl'bælənst〕*adj.* 健全的；明智的
stable〔'stebḷ〕*adj.* 安定的；穩定的
citizen〔'sɪtəzṇ〕*n.* 公民；國民
know right from wrong 分辨是非
common sense 常識；好的判斷力

5. *My parents always go the extra mile.*

parents〔'pɛrənts〕*n. pl.* 父母；雙親

extra〔'ɛkstrə〕*adj.* 額外的　　mile〔maɪl〕*n.* 英里

go the extra mile 付出更多

這句話的意思是「我的父母總是付出更多。」

go the extra mile 字面意思是「走額外的英里」，引申表示「付出更多；更加努力」，例如：

To do your duty is not enough. You must
go the extra mile.

（只做分內工作是不夠的。你必須更努力。）

He's a nice guy, always ready to *go the extra mile* for his friends.

（他是一個很好的人，總是準備好爲他的朋友付出更多。）

【duty〔'djutɪ〕*n.* 責任】

這句話也可以說成：

My parents never give up.

（我的父母從不放棄。）

My parents give everything they've got.

（我的父母付出他們的所有。）

folks〔fɔlks〕*n. pl.* 家人；雙親

give up 放棄

6. ***Their patience has no limit***.

patience〔'peʃəns〕*n.* 耐心　　limit〔'lɪmɪt〕*n.* 極限

這句話的意思是「他們的耐心沒有極限。」
也就是「他們很有耐心。」這句話也可以說成：

There is no limit to their patience.

（他們的耐心沒有極限。）

Their kindness has no bounds.

（他們的仁慈無邊無際。）

kindness〔'kaɪndnɪs〕*n.* 仁慈；好意
bounds〔baʊndz〕*n. pl.* 界限

7. ***It takes good character to raise good kids***.

take〔tek〕*v.* 需要　　character〔'kæɪktə〕*n.* 人格；品行
raise〔rez〕*v.* 撫養　　kid〔kɪd〕*n.* 小孩

這句話的意思是「需要有好的品德才能養育出好的
小孩。」養育子女，父母本身必須要有良好的品德，才
能教育出品行良好的下一代，這句話也可以說成：

Children look up to their elders.

（小孩景仰的他們的長輩。）

Children need good role models.

（小孩需要好的模範。）

look up to 尊敬；景仰
elder〔'ɛldə〕*n.* 年長者；長輩【通常用複數】
role model 模範

作文範例

2

My Parents

My parents play a big part in my life. They have raised three children, and all of us are well-adjusted. Their influence is the reason. My parents believe in communication, *so* they take time to listen to us. They understand our problems. *In addition*, my parents have good morals. They don't smoke, drink, or gamble. *Furthermore*, they demonstrate good virtue in all their actions. They teach me to have respect and to be kind to others.

One time, my sister failed a test. My parents did not scold or judge her. *Instead*, they listened to her worries. Then they simply encouraged her to try harder. Having patience is important for a parent. Being a parent is a tough job. It comes with a lot of responsibility. *In modern times*, parenting is complicated. It takes good character to raise good kids. That's why my parents make me proud to be their child.

我的父母

　　我的父母在我的人生中扮演重要的角色，他們扶養了三個小孩，而且我們都適應良好，這是因為他們的影響。我的父母相信溝通是有效的，所以他們會花時間聽我們講話。他們了解我們的問題。而且，我們父母有良好的品德。他們不抽煙、喝酒或賭博。此外，他們的行為展現出良好的美德，他們教我要尊重並善待他人。

　　有一次，我的妹妹考試不及格。我的父母並沒有責備或批評她，反而聆聽她的問題。然後他們只是鼓勵她要更努力。有耐心對一位父母來說是很重要的。為人父母是很困難的工作，這伴隨著許多責任。在現代，教育子女是很複雜的，需要良好的品德才能養育出好孩子。那就是為什麼我會覺得當我父母的小孩很自豪。

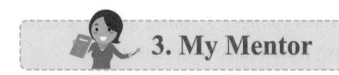

3. My Mentor

A mentor does not just offer wisdom.
A mentor inspires questions.
A mentor should help you help yourself.

3

My mentor is Ms. Chen.
She is a teacher at my school.
I have been her student for three years.

She is a great teacher.
She teaches us things we can use in school.
She also teaches us things we can use
  in life.

---

mentor (ˈmɛntɚ)

wisdom (ˈwɪzdəm)

question (ˈkwɛstʃən)

Ms. (mɪz)

student (ˈstjudn̩t)

teach (titʃ)

life (laɪf)

offer (ˈɔfɚ)

inspire (ɪnˈspaɪr)

help (hɛlp)

teacher (ˈtitʃɚ)

great (gret)

use (juz)

3

When I was younger, I wanted to be a scientist.
But now, I want to be a journalist.
It's all because of Ms. Chen.

No one has influenced me more than
　Ms. Chen.
It was in her class that I learned to love writing.
Now it's my passion.

Ms. Chen convinced me to enter a writing
　contest.
She helped me edit the story.
She was there with me every step of the way.

younger (ˈjʌŋgɚ)　　　　want (wɑnt)
scientist (ˈsaɪəntɪst)　　journalist (ˈdʒɝnḷɪst)
because of　　　　　influence (ˈɪnfluəns)
learn (lɝn)　　　　　　writing (ˈraɪtɪŋ)
passion (ˈpæʃən)　　　　convince (kənˈvɪns)
enter (ˈɛntɚ)　　　　　　contest (ˈkɑntɛst)
edit (ˈɛdɪt)　　　　　　　story (ˈstorɪ)
step (stɛp)　　　　　　***every step of the way***

Then Ms. Chen told me I had won!

I had a special reason for being happy.

I knew she was proud of my achievement.

Ms. Chen is very kind.

She is always ready to help.

She gives advice and encouragement.

Some day I will be a great writer.

Some day I will not be Ms. Chen's
    student.

But she will always be my mentor.

---

told〔 told 〕	won〔 wʌn 〕
special〔'spɛʃəl 〕	reason〔'rizn̩ 〕
happy〔'hæpɪ 〕	*be proud of*
achievement〔 ə'tʃivmənt 〕	
kind〔 kaɪnd 〕	always〔'ɔlwez 〕
ready〔'rɛdɪ 〕	advice〔 əd'vaɪs 〕
encouragement〔 ɪn'kɝɪdʒmənt 〕	
some day	writer〔'raɪtɚ 〕

3. *My Mentor*

● 演講解說

A mentor does not just offer wisdom.	良師並不只是提供智慧。
A mentor inspires questions.	良師鼓勵發問。
A mentor should help you help yourself.	良師應該幫你學會自助。
My mentor is Ms. Chen.	我的良師是陳老師。
She is a teacher at my school.	她是我學校的老師。
I have been her student for three years.	我當她的學生三年了。
She is a great teacher.	她是位很棒的老師。
She teaches us things we can use in school.	她教我們能在學校使用的事物。
She also teaches us things we can use in life.	她也教我們人生中實用的事物。

** ——————————————

mentor〔'mɛntɚ〕 *n.* 良師　　offer〔'ɔfɚ〕 *v.* 提供
wisdom〔'wɪzdəm〕 *n.* 智慧
inspire〔 ɪn'spaɪr 〕 *v.* 激勵；給予靈感
question〔'kwɛstʃən〕 *n.* 問題　　help〔 hɛlp 〕 *v.* 幫助
Ms.〔 mɪz 〕 *n.* …女士　　teacher〔'titʃɚ〕 *n.* 老師
student〔'stjudn̩t〕 *n.* 學生　　great〔 gret 〕 *adj.* 很棒的
teach〔 titʃ 〕 *v.* 教導　　use〔 juz 〕 *v.* 使用
life〔 laɪf 〕 *n.* 人生；生活

***When I was younger*, *I wanted to*
be a scientist.**
But now, I want to be a journalist.
It's all because of Ms. Chen.

No one has influenced me more
　than Ms. Chen.
It was in her class that I learned
　to love writing.
Now it's my passion.

Ms. Chen convinced me to enter
　a writing contest.
She helped me edit the story.
She was there with me every step
　of the way.

當我較年幼時，我想要當
科學家。
但是現在，我想要當記者。
這都是因為陳老師。

沒有人比陳老師影響我更
多。
就是在她的課堂上我學著
愛上寫作。
現在這是我的愛好。

陳老師說服我參加寫作
比賽。
她協助我編寫故事情節。
她一路上一直陪伴我。

3

** ——————————

younger〔ˈjʌŋɡɚ〕*adj.* 較年幼的（young 的比較級）
want〔wɑnt〕*v.* 想要　　scientist〔ˈsaɪəntɪst〕*n.* 科學家
journalist〔ˈdʒɝnḷɪst〕*n.* 記者　　***because of*** 因為
influence〔ˈɪnfluəns〕*v.* 影響　　learn〔lɝn〕*v.* 學習；學到
writing〔ˈraɪtɪŋ〕*n.* 寫作　　passion〔ˈpæʃən〕*n.* 熱情；愛好
convince〔kənˈvɪns〕*v.* 說服　　enter〔ˈɛntɚ〕*v.* 進入；參加
contest〔ˈkɑntɛst〕*n.* 比賽　　edit〔ˈɛdɪt〕*v.* 編輯
story〔ˈstorɪ〕*n.* 故事；情節　　step〔stɛp〕*n.* 一步
every step of the way 一路上

3

Then Ms. Chen told me I had | 然後陳老師告訴我，我贏
won! | 了比賽。
I had a special reason for being | 我感到高興有一個特別的
happy. | 理由。
I knew she was proud of my | 我知道她對我的成就感到
achievement. | 光榮。

Ms. Chen is very kind. | 陳老師很善良。
She is always ready to help. | 她總是願意要幫助他人。
She gives advice and | 她會提供建議並給予鼓
encouragement. | 勵。

Some day I will be a great | 將來有一天我會成為很棒
writer. | 的作家。
Some day I will not be Ms. Chen's | 將來有一天我不再是陳老
student. | 師的學生。
But she will always be my mentor. | 但她永遠是我的良師。

＊＊————————————————————————

told〔told〕v. 告訴（tell 的過去式）
won〔wʌn〕v. 贏（win 的過去式、過去分詞）
special〔'spɛʃəl〕adj. 特別的　　reason〔'rizn̩〕n. 理由；原因
happy〔'hæpɪ〕adj. 高興的　***be proud of*** 對…感到驕傲；以…為榮
achievement〔ə'tʃivmənt〕n. 成就　kind〔kaɪnd〕adj. 善良的
always〔'ɔlwɛz〕adv. 總是；一直
ready〔'rɛdɪ〕adj. 準備好的；願意的
advice〔əd'vaɪs〕n. 勸告；建議
encouragement〔ɪn'kɝɪdʒmənt〕n. 鼓勵
some day　（將來）有一天；有朝一日　　writer〔'raɪtɚ〕n. 作家

背景說明

　　人從幼稚園到小學、國中、高中，甚至到大學，會遇到許多老師。老師除了教導知識，還會告訴我們許多待人接物的進退禮儀，甚至是啟發我們的智慧。本篇演講稿，要教你如何感謝一生的良師。

3

1. *A mentor should help you help yourself.*

mentor〔'mɛntɚ〕*n.* 良師　　help〔hɛlp〕*v.* 幫助

　　這句話的意思是「良師應該幫你學會自助。」這句有個典故，原來是：

God helps those who help themselves.

（【諺】天助自助者。）

所謂「師父引進門，修行在個人。」因此本文做了一點修改來符合文旨。這句話也可以說成：

A mentor should help you realize your
　　potential.（良師應該幫助你發揮你潛力。）

A mentor should point you in the right
　　direction.（良師應該指引你走正確的方向。）

realize〔'riə‚laɪz〕*v.* 實現
potential〔pə'tɛnʃəl〕*n.* 潛力
point〔pɔɪnt〕*v.* 替～指路
right〔raɪt〕*adj.* 正確的
direction〔də'rɛkʃən〕*n.* 方向

2. *She also teaches us things we can use in life.*

teach〔titʃ〕v. 教導　　use〔juz〕v. 使用
life〔laɪf〕n. 人生；生活

　　這句話的意思是「她也教我們生活中實用的事物。」
良師之所以不只是老師，就是在於他們還可以，教導
我們生活上的事物，讓我們可以在社會上生存。這句
話也可以說成：

She also teaches life lessons.（她也教授人生經驗。）

Her teachings also have practical
　applications.

（她的教導也有實際的功用途。）

lesson〔'lɛsn̩〕n. 課程；經驗
teachings〔'titʃɪŋz〕n. pl. 教導
practical〔'præktɪkl̩〕adj. 實際的
application〔ˌæplə'keʃən〕n. 應用；用途

3. *No one has influenced me more than Ms. Chen.*

influence〔'ɪnfluəns〕v. 影響　　Ms.〔mɪz〕n. …女士

　　美國小孩稱呼老師，和中國人不一樣，中國人稱「劉
老師」，美國人不稱 Teacher Liu（誤）。男士用 Mr.，女士
不管有沒有結婚，都可以用 Ms.，如：Mr. Smith（史密斯
先生）、Ms. Parker（派克小姐）。

　　這句話的意思是「沒有人比陳老師影響我更多。」
這句話是以否定的方式來表達最高級，也就是「陳老師影
響我最多。」這句話也可以說成：

Ms. Chen made the deepest impression
　　on me. (陳老師對我造成最深的影響。)
Ms. Chen was the most influential teacher
　　I ever had. (陳老師是我的老師中最有影響力的。)

impression〔ɪm'prɛʃən〕 n. 印象；影響
make an impression on 給…印象；影響
influential〔ˌɪnflu'ɛnʃəl〕 adj. 有影響力的
ever〔'ɛvɚ〕 adv. 曾經

3

4. ***Ms. Chen convinced me to enter a writing contest.***
convince〔kən'vɪns〕 v. 說服
enter〔'ɛntɚ〕 v. 進入；參加
writing〔'raɪtɪŋ〕 adj. 寫作的　　contest〔'kɑntɛst〕 n. 比賽

這句話的意思是「陳老師說服我要參加寫作比賽。」
convince 是「說服」的意思，用法是：convince *sb.*
to V. 或是 convince *sb.* of N. 例如：

We ***convinced*** her ***to go*** with us.
（我們說服她和我們一起去。）

He tried to ***convinced*** me ***of*** his innocence.
（他試圖使我相信他是清白的。）

【innocence〔'ɪnəsn̩s〕 n. 清白】

enter 在這裡是「參加」的意思，等於 take part in 或
participate in，例如：

She has ***entered*** several poetry competitions.
（她已參加過好幾個作詩比賽。）

John ***took part in*** many school activities.

（約翰參加過很多學校的活動。）

She didn't ***participate in*** the discussion.

（她並沒有參與討論。）

participate〔 par'tɪsə,pet 〕*v.* 參加 < *in* >
several〔'sɛvərəl〕 *adj.* 幾個的   poetry〔'po·ɪtrɪ〕 *n.* 詩
competition〔,kampə'tɪʃən〕 *n.* 比賽
activity〔 æk'tɪvətɪ〕 *n.* 活動
discussion〔 dɪ'skʌʃən〕 *n.* 討論

5. ***She was there with me every step of the way.***

step〔stɛp〕 *n.* 一步   ***be there with me*** 陪伴我
every step of the way 一路上

　　這句話的意思是「她一路上一直陪伴我。」
every step of the way 字面意思是「路上的每一步」，
也就是「一路上；全程」，例如：

We worked hard together every step of the
way.（我們全程都一起努力。）

work hard 努力   together〔 tə'gɛðə 〕 *adv.* 一起

這句話也可以說成：

She was with me from start to finish.
（她從開始到結束都陪著我。）

She was at my side until the very end.
（她待在我身邊一直到最後。）

start〔 stɑrt 〕 *n.* 開始   finish〔'fɪnɪʃ〕 *n.* 結束
from start to finish 從開始到結束

side〔saɪd〕*n.* 旁邊　　until〔ən'tɪl〕*prep.* 直到
the very 最…的；就是…　　end〔ɛnd〕*n.* 結束

6. *I had a special reason for being happy.*

special〔'spɛʃəl〕*adj.* 特別的　　reason〔'rizn̩〕*n.* 理由；原因
happy〔'hæpɪ〕*adj.* 高興的

這句話的意思是「我感到高興有一個特別的理由。」
a reason for…意思是「…的理由」，是固定的用法，例如：

What's the ***reason for*** his absence?
（他缺席的理由是什麼？）
【absence〔'æbsn̩s〕*n.* 缺席】

也有 for…reason 的用法，表示「因為…」，例如：

He hit me ***for no reason***.（他平白無故就打我。）

Alice resigned ***for some reason***.
（愛麗絲因為某個原因而辭職。）

hit〔hɪt〕*v.* 打【三態為：hit-hit-hit】
resign〔rɪ'zaɪn〕*n.* 辭職　　some〔sʌm〕*adj.* 某個

這句話也可以說成：

My happiness had a special meaning.
（我的快樂有個特別的意義。）

There was more to the victory than simply
winning.（勝利除了贏，還有其他的意義。）

happiness〔'hæpɪnɪs〕*n.* 快樂；幸福
meaning〔'minɪŋ〕*n.* 意義　　victory〔'vɪktrɪ〕*n.* 勝利

3

> ***There is more to*** A ***than*** B. A 代表的不只 B。
> simply〔ˈsɪmplɪ〕*adv.* 只（= *only*）

7. *She is always ready to help*.

always〔ˈɔlwez〕*adv.* 總是；一直
ready〔ˈrɛdɪ〕*adj.* 準備好的；願意的
help〔hɛlp〕*v.* 幫助

這句話的意思是「她總是準備好要幫助他人。」
也可以說成：

She is generous with her time.
（她很慷慨願意付出時間。）

You can count on her to help anyone in need.
（你可以指望她會幫助任何需要幫助的人。）

generous〔ˈdʒɛnərəs〕*adj.* 慷慨的；大方的
be generous with 慷慨給予…；不吝嗇給予…
count on 依靠；指望（= *depend on*）
in need 需要幫助；在困難中

英文諺語裡，常常勸他人要幫助別人，這是種
美德，例如：

It's more blessed to give than to receive.
（施比受更有福。）

Charity begins at home, but should not end
there.（仁愛先從家裡開始，但不可僅此而已。）

blessed〔ˈblɛsɪd〕*adj.* 幸福的　　receive〔rɪˈsiv〕*v.* 接受
charity〔ˈtʃærətɪ〕*n.* 仁愛；慈善

○ 作文範例

My Mentor

A mentor does not just offer wisdom. A mentor helps you help yourself. My mentor is my teacher, Ms. Chen.

No one has influenced me more than Ms. Chen. *Because of* her, I want to be a journalist. It was in her class that I learned to love writing. In my first year, Ms. Chen convinced me to enter a writing contest. She helped me edit my short story. She was there with me every step of the way. It was *also* Ms. Chen who told me I had won the contest! The award was nice, *but* I was happy for another reason. I knew how proud she was of my achievement.

Since then, Ms. Chen has continued to support my writing. She is always ready to help. She gives advice and encouragement. Some day I will be a great writer. Some day I will not be Ms. Chen's student. *But* she will always be my mentor.

● 中文翻譯

我的良師

一位良師不只提供智慧，良師會幫助你自助。我的良師，是我的老師，陳老師。

沒有人對我的影響大過陳老師。因為她，我想要當一位記者。就是在她的課堂上，我學會愛上寫作。在學校的第一年，陳老師鼓勵我去參加寫作比賽。她協助我編寫我的短篇小說，她一路一直陪伴我。也是陳老師告訴我，我贏得了比賽！得獎很棒，但是我是因為另一個原因而感到快樂，我知道她是多麼地以我的成就為榮。

從那時候開始，陳老師持續支持我寫作。她總是願意要幫助我，給我建議和鼓勵。將來有一天，我會成為一位很棒的作家。將來有一天，我不再是陳老師的學生，但是她永遠是我的良師。

4. My Idol

Some of my friends idolize pop stars.
Others worship professional athletes.
However, my idol is much closer to home.

I have always looked up to my Uncle Mike.
I have admired him for all his success.
Uncle Mike is my idol.

He is the only person in my family to
   become wealthy.
He has shown me that anyone can do what
   they set their mind to.
His success has given me hope that one day,
   I too, can live a good life.

4

---

idol (ˈaɪdḷ)
pop (pɑp)
worship (ˈwɝʃəp)
athlete (ˈæθlɪt)
look up to
success (səkˈsɛs)
shown (ʃon)
hope (hop)

idolize (ˈaɪdḷˌaɪz)
star (stɑr)
professional (prəˈfɛʃənḷ)
close to home
admire (ədˈmaɪr)
wealthy (ˈwɛlθɪ)
set one's mind to
live a…life

Uncle Mike has inspired me to set goals.
He encourages me to aim higher
and higher.
He never lets me take the easy way out.

Uncle Mike's success amazes me.
It baffles me how he did it.
Only a special person can do what he did.

Our family was never rich.
Everybody worked very hard.
Nothing was ever given to us.

inspire〔ɪn'spaɪr〕   set〔sɛt〕
goal〔gol〕   encourage〔ɪn'kɝɪdʒ〕
aim〔em〕   *aim high*
take〔tek〕   easy〔'izɪ〕
way out   amaze〔ə'mez〕
baffle〔'bæfl̩〕   special〔'spɛʃəl〕
rich〔rɪtʃ〕   work〔wɝk〕
hard〔hɑrd〕   ever〔'ɛvɚ〕
given〔'gɪvən〕

Uncle Mike created his company from the
  ground up.
It took him ten years, but it finally paid off.
He sold it for two hundred million dollars!

Uncle Mike set an example.
With determination, I can accomplish
  anything.
Nothing can stop me.

Uncle Mike has always believed in me.
He has supported everything I do.
He gives me the inspiration I need.

4

---

create (krɪ'et)   company ('kʌmpənɪ)
from the ground up   took (tʊk)
finally ('faɪnḷɪ)   *paid off*
sold (sold)   example (ɪg'zæmpḷ)
determination (dɪ,tɜmə'neʃən)
accomplish (ə'kɑmplɪʃ)   stop (stɑp)
believe (bə'liv)   support (sə'port)
inspiration (,ɪnspə'reʃən)   need (nid)

4. *My Idol*

演講解說

Some of my friends idolize pop stars.	我有些朋友崇拜流行明星。
Others worship professional athletes.	有些崇拜專業運動員。
However, my idol is much closer to home	然而,我的偶像對我有更直接的影響。
I have always looked up to my Uncle Mike.	我一直都很尊敬我的叔叔麥可。
I have admired him for all his success.	我欽佩他的成功。
Uncle Mike is my idol.	麥可叔叔就是我的偶像。
He is the only person in my family to become wealthy.	他是我們家族裡唯一變富有的人。
He has shown me that anyone can do what they set their mind to.	他向我證明了任何人都可以做到他一心想做的事。
His success has given me hope that one day, I too, can live a good life.	他的成功給了我希望,有一天,我也可以過好生活。

**────────────────

idol〔ˈaɪdḷ〕 *n.* 偶像　　*some…others*~ 有些…有些~

idolize〔ˈaɪdḷˌaɪz〕 *v.* 視…為偶像;崇拜

pop〔pɑp〕 *adj.* 流行的 (= *popular*)　　star〔stɑr〕 *n.* 明星

worship〔ˈwɝʃɪp〕 *n.* 崇拜　　professional〔prəˈfɛʃənḷ〕 *adj.* 專業的

athlete〔ˈæθlit〕 *n.* 運動員　　*close to home* 有直接的影響

look up to 尊敬　　admire〔ədˈmaɪr〕 *v.* 欽佩;讚賞

success〔səkˈsɛs〕 *n.* 成功　　wealthy〔ˈwɛlθɪ〕 *adj.* 富有的

shown〔ʃon〕 *v.* 給~看;向~證明 (show 的過去分詞)

set one's mind to 致力於;專心做　　hope〔hop〕 *n.* 希望

live a…life 過…的生活

Uncle Mike has inspired me to set goals.	麥可叔叔激勵我要設定目標。
He encourages me to aim higher and higher.	他鼓勵我要力爭上游。
He never lets me take the easy way out.	他從不讓我走捷徑。
Uncle Mike's success amazes me.	麥可叔叔的成功讓我感到驚訝。
It baffles me how he did it.	我對他是如何做到的感到困惑。
Only a special person can do what he did.	只有特別的人才能像他一樣做到。
Our family was never rich.	我們從來都不是有錢人家。
Everybody worked very hard.	每個人都很努力。
Nothing was ever given to us.	我們從未不勞而獲。

4

** ————————

inspire〔ɪn'spaɪr〕v. 激勵　set〔sɛt〕v. 設定
goal〔gol〕n. 目標　encourage〔ɪn'kɜɪdʒ〕v. 鼓勵
aim〔em〕v. 訂定目標；企圖　***aim high*** 胸懷大志；力爭上游
take〔tek〕v. 選取；利用　easy〔'izɪ〕adj. 容易的
way out 出路；方法　amaze〔ə'mez〕v. 使驚訝
baffle〔'bæfl̩〕v. 使困惑　special〔'spɛʃəl〕adj. 特別的
rich〔rɪtʃ〕adj. 有錢的　work〔wɜk〕v. 工作
hard〔hɑrd〕adv. 努力地　***work hard*** 努力
given〔'gɪvən〕v. 給（give 的過去分詞）

Uncle Mike created his company from the ground up.	麥可叔叔從頭開始創立公司。
It took him ten years, but it finally paid off.	這花了他十年，但他最後成功了。
He sold it for two hundred million dollars!	他的公司以兩億美元賣出！
Uncle Mike set an example.	麥可叔叔樹立了榜樣。
With determination, I can accomplish anything.	如果有決心，我就可以完成任何事情。
Nothing can stop me.	沒有事情可以阻撓我。
Uncle Mike has always believed in me.	麥可叔叔一直都很信任我。
He has supported everything I do.	我支持所有我做的事情。
He gives me the inspiration I need.	他給我所需要的啓發。

**

create〔krɪ'et〕v. 創造　　company〔'kʌmpənɪ〕n. 公司
from the ground up 從頭開始
took〔tʊk〕v. 花（時間）（take 的過去式）
finally〔'faɪnḷɪ〕adv. 最後；終於　　***pay off*** 成功
sold〔sold〕v. 賣（sell 的過去式）　　set〔sɛt〕v. 樹立（三態同形）
example〔ɪg'zæmpḷ〕n. 例子；榜樣
determination〔dɪ,tɜmə'neʃən〕n. 決心
accomplish〔ə'kɑmplɪʃ〕v. 完成　　stop〔stɑp〕v. 停止；阻止
believe〔bə'liv〕v. 相信　　***believe in*** 信任
support〔sə'port〕v. 支持
inspiration〔,ɪnspə'reʃən〕n. 激勵；啓發　　need〔nid〕v. 需要

● 背景說明

　　從小到大，我們都會有不同的偶像，他們在我們各個生命的階段，都有或多或少的影響，我們也因此有模仿他們的傾向。本篇演講稿，要教你如何描述自己的偶像，以及他對你的影響。

1. ***However, my idol is much closer to home.***

however〔hauˈɛvə〕*adv.* 然而；不過
idol〔ˈaɪdl̩〕*n.* 偶像
much〔mʌtʃ〕*adv.*（修飾比較級）非常
be close to home 有直接的影響

　　這句話的意思是「然而，我的偶像對我有更直接的影響。」be close to home 字面意思是「靠近家」，引申為「接近；直接」，這裡的意思就是「有直接的影響」（= *have a direct personal impact*），例如：

This problem *is* particularly *close to home*
　for many parents.
（這個問題對很多父母來說，有切身的影響。）

Her remarks *were* a bit too *close to home*.
（她的評論有點太直接了。）

problem〔ˈprɑbləm〕*n.* 問題
particularly〔pəˈtɪkjələlɪ〕*v.* 特別；尤其
parents〔ˈpɛrənts〕*n. pl.* 父母；雙親
remark〔rɪˈmɑrk〕*n.* 評論；話

4

這句話也可說成：

However, my hero is from my everyday life.

（然而，我的英雄是來自我每天的生活。）

However, my idol is more of a normal person.

（然而，我的偶像比較像是一般人。）

hero〔ˈhɪro〕*n.* 英雄；崇拜的人
everyday〔ˈɛvrɪˌde〕*adj.* 每天的
be more of 比較像是…
normal〔ˈnɔrml̩〕*adj.* 正常的；普通的

4

2. *He has shown me that anyone can do what they set their mind to.*

shown〔ʃon〕*v.* 給～看；向～證明（show 的過去分詞）
set one's mind to 致力於；專心做

　　這句話的意思是「他向我證明了任何人都可以做到他一心想做的事。」set *one's* mind to 字面意思是「把某人的心放在…上」，所以就是「致力於；專心做」，動詞也可以改成 put 或 turn，例如：

You can do anything if you *put your mind to* it.

（如果你專心做一件事，你就可以完成它。）

這句話也可說成：

He made it clear that I can achieve anything.

（他清楚說明我可以完成任何事情。）

He proved to me clear that anything is possible.

（他向我清楚證明了，任何事都是可能的。）

clear〔klɪr〕 *adj.* 清楚的
make it clear that 明確表示
achieve〔əˋtʃiv〕 *v.* 完成；實現
prove〔pruv〕 *v.* 證明
possible〔ˋpɑsəbḷ〕 *adj.* 可能的

3. ***He encourages me to aim higher and higher.***

encourage〔ɪnˋkɝɪdʒ〕 *v.* 鼓勵
aim〔em〕 *v.* 訂定目標；企圖
high〔haɪ〕 *adv.* 高高地
aim high 胸懷大志；力爭上游

4

這句話的意思是「他鼓勵我要力爭上游。」aim high 字面意思是「目標設得高」，也就是「胸懷大志；力爭上游」；「比較級＋比較級」表示「越來越…」，所以 higher and higher 是指「越來越高」。同義的說法：be ambitious, think big。

Must women who ***aim high*** be more
　　hard-working than men?

（胸懷大志的女人一定要比男人還努力嗎？）

Boys, ***be ambitious***!

（孩子們，要胸懷大志！）

When it comes to starting your own business,
　　it can pay to ***think big***.

（一說到要自己創業，胸懷大志是值得的。）

ambitious〔æm'bɪʃəs〕*adj.* 有野心的；有抱負的
think big 胸懷大志
hard-working〔ˌhɑrd'wɝkɪŋ〕*adj.* 努力的；勤勉的
when it comes to V-ing 一提到
it pays to V. …是值得的   ***start a business*** 創業

這句話也可說成：

He supports me whatever I choose to do.
（他支持任何我選擇要做的任何事。）

He pushes me to achieve great things.
（他鼓勵我去完成偉大的事。）

support〔sə'port〕*v.* 支持   choose〔tʃuz〕*v.* 選擇
push〔puʃ〕*v.* 支持；鼓勵

4. *He never lets me take the easy way out.*

let sb. + V. 讓某人…   take〔tek〕*v.* 選取；利用
easy〔'izɪ〕*adj.* 容易的   ***way out*** 出路；方法

這句話字面意思是「他從不讓我選取容易的出路。」其實就是「他從不讓我走捷徑。」way out 原本是「出口」（= *exit*），這裡引申為「方法」（= *solution*），例如：

He blocked the ***way out***.（他擋住了出口。）

There must be a ***way out*** of this mess.
（一定有一個處理這麻煩的方法。）

exit〔'ɛgzɪt〕*n.* 出口   mess〔mɛs〕*n.* 混亂；麻煩

這句話也可說成：

> He always keeps me focused on the tasks
>   at hand.
>
> （他總是使我專注在我手邊的工作。）

> He never lets me quit on an endeavor.
>
> （他從不讓我放棄努力。）

> ***keep** sb.~*　使某人~
> focused〔'fokəst〕*adj.* 專心的 *< on >*
> task〔tæsk〕*n.* 工作
> ***at hand***　在手邊
> ***quit on***　放棄（*= give up on*）
> endeavor〔ɪn'dɛvə〕*n.* 努力

5. *Nothing was ever given to us.*

ever〔'ɛvə〕*adv.*【用於否定句】（不）曾
given〔'gɪvən〕*v.* 給（give 的過去分詞）

　　　這句話字面的意思是「從來沒有東西是給我們的。」
引申為「我們從未不勞而獲。」，也可以說成：

> Nothing was ever handed to us.
>
> （沒有事物是伸手就有的。）

> We had to earn everything we got.
>
> （我們所有的東西都是努力得來的。）

> hand〔hænd〕*v.* 拿給；遞給
> earn〔ɝn〕*v.* 賺取；（經努力而）獲得

6. *Uncle Mike created his company from the ground up*.

create〔krɪˋet〕*v.* 創造　　company〔ˋkʌmpənɪ〕*n.* 公司

from the ground up 從頭開始

　　　　這句話字面的意思是「麥可叔叔從地面開始創造他的公司。」引申為「麥可叔叔從頭開始創立公司。」from the ground up 就是中文「萬丈高樓平地起」的意思。這句話也可以說成：

Uncle Mike built his company from scratch.

（麥可叔叔從頭開始建立公司。）

Uncle Mike is a self-made businessman.

（麥可叔叔是個白手起家的商人。）

built〔bɪlt〕*v.* 建立（build 的過去式）
from scratch 從頭開始；從零開始【例如：
start from scratch（從一無所有開始；白手起家）】
self-made〔ˋsɛlfˋmed〕*adj.* 白手起家的
businessman〔ˋbɪznɪsˏmæn〕*n.* 商人

7. *Uncle Mike set an example*.

set〔sɛt〕*v.* 設立；樹立（三態同形）
example〔ɪgˋzæmpl̩〕*n.* 例子；榜樣

　　　　這句話的意思是「麥可叔叔樹立榜樣。」也可說成：

Uncle Mike is a role model.（麥可叔叔是模範。）

Uncle Mike set a precedent for others to follow.

（麥可叔叔立下了前例讓他人遵循。）

role model 模範　　precedent〔ˋprɛsədənt〕*n.* 前例
follow〔ˋfɑlo〕*v.* 遵循

○作文範例

My Idol

Heroes come in all sizes and shapes. *Some* of my friends idolize pop stars. *Others* worship professional athletes. *However*, my idol is much closer to home. I have always looked up to my Uncle Mike. He is the only person in my family to make it big. Our family was never rich. Uncle Mike created his company from the ground up. It took him ten years, *but* it finally paid off. Last year he sold it for two hundred million dollars!

Uncle Mike set an example. He has shown me that anyone can do what he sets his mind to. His success has given me hope that one day, I too, can live a good life. I know I can accomplish anything I set my mind to if I am determined. Uncle Mike has given me the inspiration I need to attain any goal I set for myself.

4

●中文翻譯

我的偶像

　　有形形色色的英雄，我的一些朋友把流行明星視為偶像，有些則崇拜專業運動員。然而，我的偶像對我有非常直接的影響。我一直都很尊敬麥可叔叔，他是我們家族裡唯一成功的人。我們從來都不是有錢人家。麥可叔叔白手起家，創立他的公司。這花了他十年的時間，但他最後成功了。去年，他以兩億美元把公司賣出去了！

　　麥可叔叔樹立了榜樣，他向我證明了任何人都可以做他一心想做的事。他的成功給了我希望，將來有一天，我也可以過很好的生活。我知道只要我有決心，我就可以完成任何我所專心做的任何事情。麥可叔叔給了我所需要的鼓勵，來達成我為自己設定的目標。

5. My Buddy

5

It is very hard to find a true and honest friend.
I am very lucky that I have a good buddy.
His name is James.

James is very friendly.
He is also is a good person.
He has all the qualities we seek in a buddy.

James is a very helpful person.
For instance, he helps his parents at home.
He mows the lawn and cleans the house.

buddy (ˈbʌdɪ)	hard (hɑrd)
true (tru)	honest (ˈɑnɪst)
lucky (ˈlʌkɪ)	friendly (ˈfrɛndlɪ)
person (ˈpɝsn̩)	quality (ˈkwɑlətɪ)
seek (sik)	helpful (ˈhɛlpfəl)
for instance	help (hɛlp)
parents (ˈpɛrənts)	*at home*
mow (mo)	lawn (lɔn)
clean (klin)	house (haʊs)

5

James is hardworking and punctual.
He likes doing his work on time.
For example, his homework is never late.

James always attends his classes.
He is always prepared for his tests.
He works part-time to have pocket money.

Finally, James is very honest.
He speaks the truth and hates lying.
When he makes a mistake, he always
    admits to it.

hardworking (ˌhɑrd'wɝkɪŋ)
punctual ('pʌŋktʃʊəl)　　　　　work (wɝk)
on time　　　　　　　　　　*for example*
homework ('hom,wɝk)　　　　late (let)
attend (ə'tɛnd)　　　　　　class (klæs)
prepared (prɪ'pɛrd)　　　　test (tɛst)
part-time ('pɑrt'taɪm)　　　　*pocket money*
finally ('faɪnlɪ)　　　　　　*speak the truth*
hate (het)　　　　　　　　lying ('laɪɪŋ)
make a mistake　　　　　　admit (əd'mɪt)

Having a buddy like James is important.
He is a good person to be around.
He helps me stay on track.

We do things outside of school, too.
Sometimes we play sports.
Sometimes we go to the movies.

In conclusion, James is a great buddy.
He makes everyone very comfortable.
He will never let you down.

5

---

like (laɪk)   important (ɪm'pɔrtn̩t)
around (ə'raʊnd)   stay (ste)
track (træk)   *on track*
outside of   sometimes ('sʌm,taɪmz)
play (ple)   sports (spɔrts)
go to the movies   *in conclusion*
great (gret)   make (mek)
comfortable ('kʌmfə·təbl̩)
let sb. down

5. *My Buddy*

● 演講解說

It is very hard to find a true and honest friend.	要找到一位眞誠的朋友是很困難的。
I am very lucky that I have a good buddy.	我很幸運，我有一位好伙伴。
His name is James.	他叫作詹姆士。
James is very friendly.	詹姆士很友善。
He is also is a good person.	他也是個好人。
He has all the qualities we seek in a buddy.	他有所有我們想在伙伴身上找到的特質。
James is a very helpful person.	詹姆士非常樂於助人。
For instance, he helps his parents at home.	舉例來說，他在家會幫助父母。
He mows the lawn and cleans the house.	他會割草坪的草和打掃家裡。

**

buddy〔ˋbʌdɪ〕*n.* 兄弟；伙伴　　hard〔hɑrd〕*adj.* 困難的
true〔tru〕*adj.* 忠實的；忠誠的　　lucky〔ˋlʌkɪ〕*adj.* 幸運的
good〔gʊd〕*adj.* 好的；善良的　　friendly〔ˋfrɛndlɪ〕*adj.* 友善的
person〔ˋpɜsṇ〕*n.* 人　　quality〔ˋkwɑlətɪ〕*n.* 特質
seek〔sik〕*v.* 尋找　　helpful〔ˋhɛlpfəl〕*adj.* 熱於助人的
for instance 舉例來說　　help〔hɛlp〕*v.* 幫助
parents〔ˋpɛrənts〕*n. pl.* 父母　　*at home* 在家
mow〔mo〕*v.* 割（草）　　lawn〔lɔn〕*n.* 草坪
clean〔mo〕*v.* 清理；打掃　　house〔haʊs〕*n.* 房子

James is hardworking and punctual.　詹姆士勤奮又準時。
He likes doing his work on time.　他喜歡準時做他的工作。
For example, his homework is　舉例來說，他從不遲交作
　　never late.　業。

James always attends his classes.　詹姆士上課都會出席。
He is always prepared for his tests.　他總是為考試做好準備。
He works part-time to have pocket　他做兼職的工作來賺取零
　　money.　用錢。

Finally, James is very honest.　最後，詹姆士很誠實。
He speaks the truth and hates lying.　他說實話，討厭說謊。
When he makes a mistake, he　當他犯錯，他一定會承
　　always admits to it.　認。

5

** ──────────────────

hardworking〔,hɑrd'wɝkɪŋ〕*adj.* 勤奮的
punctual〔'pʌŋktʃuəl〕*adj.* 準時的
work〔wɝk〕*n.* 工作　　***on time*** 準時地
for example 舉例來說　　homework〔'hom,wɝk〕*n.* 家庭作業
late〔let〕*adj.* 遲的　　attend〔ə'tɛnd〕*v.* 出席；上（學）
class〔klæs〕*n.* 課　　prepared〔prɪ'pɛrd〕*adj.* 準備好的
test〔tɛst〕*n.* 測驗；考試　　part-time〔'pɑrt'taɪm〕*adv.* 兼職地
pocket money 零用錢　　finally〔'faɪnlɪ〕*adv.* 最後
speak the truth 說實話　　hate〔het〕*v.* 討厭
lying〔'laɪɪŋ〕*v.* 說謊（lie 的動名詞）　　***make a mistake*** 犯錯
admit〔əd'mɪt〕*v.* 承認 < to >

Having a buddy like James is important.
有一個像詹姆士這樣的伙伴是很重要的。

He is a good person to be around.
有他這樣的人在身邊很好。

He helps me stay on track.
他幫助我步入正軌。

We do things outside of school, too.
我們也會在校外做其他事情。

Sometimes we play sports.
我們有時候做運動。

Sometimes we go to the movies.
我們有時候去看電影。

In conclusion, James is a great buddy.
總之,詹姆士是位好伙伴。

He makes everyone very comfortable.
他讓每個人都感到舒服。

He will never let you down.
他永遠不會讓你失望。

**

like 〔 laɪk 〕 *prep.* 像　　important 〔 ɪm'pɔrtn̩t 〕 *adj.* 重要的
around 〔 ə'raʊnd 〕 *prep.* 和…附近;在…的身邊
stay 〔 ste 〕 *v.* 保持　　**on track** 在軌道上;按部就班
outside of 在…的外面
sometimes 〔 'sʌmˌtaɪmz 〕 *adv.* 有時候　　play 〔 ple 〕 *v.* 玩
sports 〔 spɔrts 〕 *n. pl.* 運動　　**play sports** 做運動
go to the movies 去看電影　　**in conclusion** 總之
make 〔 mek 〕 *v.* 使　　comfortable 〔 'kʌmfətəbl̩ 〕 *adj.* 舒服的
let *sb.* **down** 使某人失望

●背景說明

　　從小到大，會交到很多朋友，不管是在學校、社團或是各種交際活動。其中，可能會遇到和我們志趣相投的伙伴，比一般的朋友更加了解彼此。本篇演講稿，要教你如何介紹好伙伴。

1. ***I am very lucky that I have a good buddy.***

lucky〔ˈlʌkɪ〕*adj.* 幸運的

buddy〔ˈbʌdɪ〕*n.* 兄弟；伙伴

　　這句話的意思是「我很幸運我有一位好伙伴。」buddy 的發音要注意，跟 body〔ˈbɑdɪ〕*n.* 身體，很像，所以也要小心不要拼錯字了。

這句話也可以說成：

I am very fortunate to have a buddy.

（我很幸運可以有一位伙伴。）

It's my good fortune to have a trusted confidant.

（我很幸運能有一位可以信任的知己。）

fortunate〔ˈfɔrtʃənɪt〕*adj.* 幸運的

fortune〔ˈfɔrtʃən〕*n.* 運氣

trusted〔ˈtrʌstɪd〕*adj.* 可信任的

confidant〔͵kɑnfəˈdænt , ˈkɑnfə͵dænt〕*n.* 知己

2. *He has all the qualities we seek in a buddy*.

quality〔'kwɑlətɪ〕*n.* 特質　　seek〔sik〕*v.* 尋找

　　　這句話的字面意思是「他有所有我們想在伙伴
身上找到的特質。」也就是「他是個很完美的伙伴。」
這句話也可以說成：

He's everything you want in a friend.
（你想要在朋友身上找到的他都有。）

He's a perfect example of what a good
　　friend should be.
（他是完美的範例，好朋友該有的特點都有了。）

perfect〔'pɜfɪkt〕*adj.* 完美的
example〔ɪg'zæmpḷ〕*n.* 範例；榜樣

　　　另外，quality 有個很相似的字 quantity
〔'kwɑntətɪ〕*n.* 數量，要小心不要搞錯了；而且
quality 也可以當形容詞用，作「高級的」解。

The wallet is made of *quality* leather.
（這皮夾是用高級的皮革製成的。）

I prefer *quality* to *quantity*.（我重質不重量。）

I have a large *quantity* of books.
（我有大量的書。）

be made of 用…製成
quality〔'kwɑlətɪ〕*adj.* 優良的；高級的
leather〔'lɛðɚ〕*n.* 皮革　　prefer〔prɪ'fɜ〕*v.* 比較喜歡
prefer A *to* B　喜歡 A 甚於 B
a large quantity of 大量的

5

3. *For example, his homework is never late.*

for example 舉例來說

homework〔'hom͵wɝk〕*n.* 家庭作業　　late〔let〕*adj.* 遲的

　　這句話的意思是「舉例來說，他從不遲交作業。」
這句話也可以寫成：

　　For instance, he's never missed a deadline
　　　on an assignment.
　　（舉例來說，他從來不會錯過作業的期限。）

　　In fact, his homework is always finished ahead
　　　of time.（事實上，他的作業總是提前完成。）

　　for instance 舉例來說（ = *for example* ）
　　miss〔mɪs〕*v.* 錯過
　　deadline〔'dɛd͵laɪn〕*n.* 截止日期；最後期限
　　assignment〔ə'saɪnmənt〕*n.* 作業
　　in fact 事實上
　　finish〔'fɪnɪʃ〕*v.* 完成
　　ahead of time 提早
　　　（ = *beforehand* ）

4. *He speaks the truth and hates lying.*

speak〔spik〕*v.* 說　　　truth〔truθ〕*n.* 事實；眞相
hate〔het〕*v.* 討厭　　　lying〔'laɪɪŋ〕*v.* 說謊（lie 的現在分詞）

　　這句話的意思是「他說實話，討厭說謊。」誠實
是種美德，英文諺語裡面也有說：

　　Honesty is the best policy.（誠實爲上策。）

　　honesty〔'ɑnɪstɪ〕*n.* 誠實　　　policy〔'pɑləsɪ〕*n.* 政策

這句話也可以說成：

He always speaks the truth and doesn't
    exaggerate.

（他總是說實話，不會誇大。）

He honors veracity and detests a liar.

（他很誠實並且厭惡說謊的人。）

exaggerate〔ɪgˈzædʒəˌret〕v. 誇大
honor〔ˈɑnɚ〕v. 實踐；履行
veracity〔vəˈræsətɪ〕n. 誠實
detest〔dɪˈtɛst〕v. 厭惡   liar〔ˈlaɪɚ〕n. 說謊者

5

另外，lie 的三態隨著意思不同有不同的變化：

lie-lied-lied-lying v. 說謊
lie-lay-lain-lying v. 躺；位於
lay-laid-laid-laying v. 放置；下（蛋）；奠定

5. *He is a good person to be around.*

person〔ˈpɜsn̩〕n. 人
around〔əˈraʊnd〕prep. 在…的周圍；在…的身邊

這句話字面的意思是「他是個
好人，有他在他身邊很好。」就是
「有他這樣的好人在身邊很好。」
around 在這裡的意思是「在…的

周圍；在…的身邊」，而 to be around 是不定詞片語，
做形容詞用，修飾 person。這句話也可以說成：

He's fun to be with. (跟他在一起很有趣。)

I enjoy his company. (我喜歡他的陪伴。)

fun〔fʌn〕*adj.* 有趣的　　enjoy〔ɪn'dʒɔɪ〕*v.* 享受；喜歡
company〔'kʌmpənɪ〕*n.* 陪伴

6. *He helps me stay on track.*

help〔hɛlp〕*v.* 幫助
stay〔ste〕*v.* 保持
on track 在軌道上；按部就班

　　這句話字面的意思是「他幫助我保持在軌道上。」
也就是「他幫我步入正軌。」help 的用法是：help *sb.*
(to) V. (幫助某人~)，這句話省略了 to；on track 原本
的意思是「在軌道上」，引伸為「依循計畫；按部就班」，
常和 keep / get 連用，例如：

Try to keep these procedures *on track* this time.

(這一次試著要讓這些程序依照計畫執行。)

Please get this discussion *on track*.

(請讓討論依照計畫進行。)

procedure〔prə'sidʒɚ〕*n.* 程序
this time 這次　　discussion〔dɪ'skʌʃən〕*n.* 討論

這句話也可以說成：

He keeps me grounded. (他使我一直腳踏實地。)

He helps me maintain focus. (幫助我目標一致。)

grounded〔'graʊndɪd〕*adj.* 腳踏實地的
maintain〔men'ten〕*v.* 持續；保持
focus〔'fokəs〕*n.* 焦點；目標

7. ***He will never let you down.***

  let *sb.* ***down*** 讓某人失望

　　　　這句話的意思是「他永遠不會讓你失望。」
　　let *sb.* down 的意思是「讓某人失望」，也有名詞
　　的用法：a let-down（讓人失望的事），例如：

　　Don't worry. I won't ***let you down.***
　　（別擔心。我不會讓你失望的。）

　　The movie was ***a let-down.***
　　（那部電影真是讓人失望。）

　　What ***a let-down***!
　　（這真是太令人失望了！）

　　【worry〔ˈwɝi〕*v.* 擔心】

　　這句話也可以說成：

　　You can always count on him.
　　（你可以永遠依靠他。）

　　He will always be at your side.
　　（他會永遠在你身邊。）

　　count on 依靠；指望（= *depend on*）
　　be at *one's* ***side*** 在某人身邊

○ 作文範例

My Buddy

Choosing friends wisely is an important part of life. *However*, it is very hard to find a true and honest friend. I am very lucky that I have a good buddy. His name is James.

James has all the qualities we seek in a buddy. *First of all*, he is very friendly. *In addition*, James is a very helpful person. At home he helps his parents by mowing the lawn and cleaning the house. *In addition*, James is hardworking and punctual. *For example*, he always attends his classes and his homework is never late. He *also* works part-time to have pocket money. *Finally*, James is very honest. He speaks the truth and hates lying. *When* he makes a mistake, he always admits to it.

Having a buddy like James is important. I admire his character and try to follow his lead. Everything just seems a little better when he's around.

5

● 中文翻譯

我的伙伴

慎選朋友是人生中一個重要的課題。然而，要找到一個真誠的朋友真的很困難。我很幸運我有一個好伙伴，他的名字叫作詹姆士。

詹姆士有所有我們想在伙伴身上找到的特質。首先，他很友善。此外，詹姆士熱於助人。在家裡，他會幫父母除草和打掃家裡。不只如此，詹姆士勤奮又準時。舉例來說，他總是準時上課，而且從不遲交作業。他也會兼職賺點零用錢。最後，詹姆士很誠實。他說實話，討厭說謊。當他犯錯時，他都會承認。

有一個像詹姆士這樣的伙伴是很重要的。我欣賞他的人格並以他為榜樣。有他在身邊，一切事情似乎都變得更好了。

6. My Happiest Moment

Every life has its ups and downs.
Sorrow and joy are two parts of life.
In fact, life is full of good and bad.

Some things are forgotten.
Others leave a lasting impression.
We will never forget them.

Such a moment came to me last year.
I received a perfect score on my examinations.
It was the happiest moment of my life.

6

happiest ('hæpɪɪst)	moment ('momənt)
life (laɪf)	***ups and downs***
sorrow ('saro)	joy (dʒɔɪ)
part (part)	***in fact***
be full of	***good and bad***
some…others	forgotten (fə'gatṇ)
leave (liv)	lasting ('læstɪŋ)
impression (ɪm'prɛʃən)	***come to***
receive (rɪ'siv)	perfect ('pɝfɪkt)
score (skor)	examination (ɪg͵zæmə'neʃən)

***Before the exams**, **I was very nervous**.*
When I learned the result, I was so relieved.
I felt like I had won the whole world.

To celebrate, my friends and I went for
　a picnic.
The picnic spot was crowded.
We enjoyed our snacks.

We danced and sang songs.
But there was a loud cry from the lake.
A small boy was drowning in the water!

---

nervous ('nɝvəs)　　　　learn (lɝn)
result (rɪ'zʌlt)　　　　relieved (rɪ'livd)
feel like　　　　　　won (wʌn)
whole (hol)　　　　　world (wɝld)
celebrate ('sɛlə,bret)　　picnic ('pɪknɪk)
go for a picnic　　　　spot (spɑt)
crowded ('kraʊdɪd)　　　enjoy (ɪn'dʒɔɪ)
snack (snæk)　　　　　dance (dæns)
sang (sæŋ)　　　　　song (sɔŋ)
loud (laʊd)　　　　　cry (kraɪ)
lake (lek)　　　　　drown (draʊn)

***Fortunately**, **I am a good swimmer**.*

Immediately, I jumped into the lake.

After a great struggle, I pulled the boy from
the water.

The boy was in bad shape but alive.

We were all overjoyed.

Saving his life was awesome.

This event taught me a lesson.

I realized how precious life is.

That was my happiest moment.

6

---

fortunately ('fɔrtʃənɪtlɪ)	good (gʊd)
swimmer ('swɪmɚ)	
immediately (ɪ'midɪɪtlɪ)	jump (dʒʌmp)
great (gret)	struggle ('strʌgl̩)
pull (pʊl)	***in bad shape***
alive (ə'laɪv)	
overjoyed (,ovɚ'dʒɔɪd)	save (sev)
awesome ('ɔsəm)	event (ɪ'vɛnt)
taught (tɔt)	lesson ('lɛsn̩)
realize ('riə,laɪz)	precious ('prɛʃəs)

6. *My Happiest Moment*

⚪ 演講解說

Every life has its ups and downs.	人生有高潮有低潮。
Sorrow and joy are two parts of life.	悲傷和快樂是生命的兩個部分。
In fact, life is full of good and bad.	事實上，人生充滿著好事和壞事。
Some things are forgotten.	有些事情會被遺忘。
Others leave a lasting impression.	有些會留下長久的印象。
We will never forget them.	我們絕對不會忘記。
Such a moment came to me last year.	這樣的時刻發生在去年。
I received a perfect score on my examinations.	我考試得到滿分。
It was the happiest moment of my life.	那是我一生的幸福時刻。

** ────────────────

happiest〔ˈhæpɪɪst〕*adj.* 最快樂的；幸福的

moment〔ˈmomənt〕*n.* 時刻　　life〔laɪf〕*n.* 人生；生命

ups and downs 起伏；興衰　　sorrow〔ˈsaro〕*n.* 悲傷

joy〔dʒɔɪ〕*n.* 快樂　　part〔part〕*n.* 部分　　*in fact* 事實上

be full of 充滿　　*good and bad* 好壞；優劣

some…others 有些…有些

forgotten〔fəˈgatn̩〕*v.* 忘記（forget 的過去分詞）　　leave〔liv〕*v.* 留下

lasting〔ˈlæstɪŋ〕*adj.* 長久的　　impression〔ɪmˈprɛʃən〕*n.* 印象

come to 降臨；發生　　receive〔rɪˈsiv〕*v.* 收到

perfect〔ˈpɜfɪkt〕*adj.* 完美的　　score〔skor〕*n.* 分數

examination〔ɪɡˌzæməˈneʃən〕*n.* 考試

Before the exams**, **I was very nervous.	考試前，我很緊張。
When I learned the result, I was so relieved.	當我知道考試結果時，我鬆了一口氣。
I felt like I had won the whole world.	我覺得我好像贏得了全世界。
To celebrate, my friends and I went for a picnic.	為了慶祝，我朋友和我去野餐。
The picnic spot was crowded.	野餐的地點很擁擠。
We enjoyed our snacks.	我們享用我們的點心。
We danced and sang songs.	我們跳舞又唱歌。
But there was a loud cry from the lake.	但是從湖那邊傳來了很大的叫聲。
A small boy was drowning in the water!	有一個小男孩快要在水裡溺死了！

6

** ————————————————————

nervous〔'nɝvəs〕*adj.* 緊張的　　learn〔lɝn〕*v.* 知道
result〔rɪ'zʌlt〕*n.* 結果　　relieved〔rɪ'livd〕*adj.* 鬆了一口氣的
feel like 覺得好像　　won〔wʌn〕*v.* 贏得（win 的過去式和過去分詞）
whole〔hol〕*adj.* 全部的　　world〔wɝld〕*n.* 世界
celebrate〔'sɛlə,bret〕*v.* 慶祝　　picnic〔'pɪknɪk〕*n.* 野餐
go for a picnic 去野餐　　spot〔spɑt〕*n.* 地點
crowded〔'kraʊdɪd〕*adj.* 擁擠的　　enjoy〔ɪn'dʒɔɪ〕*v.* 享用
snack〔snæk〕*n.* 點心　　dance〔dæns〕*v.* 跳舞
sang〔sæŋ〕*v.* 唱歌（sing 的過去式）　　song〔sɔŋ〕*n.* 歌
loud〔laʊd〕*adj.* （聲音）大的　　cry〔kraɪ〕*n.* 叫聲
lake〔lek〕*n.* 湖　　drown〔draʊn〕*v.* 溺死；溺水

Fortunately, I am a good swimmer.	幸好，我很會游泳。
Immediately, I jumped into the lake.	我立即跳到湖裡。
After a great struggle, I pulled the boy from the water.	費了一番力後，我把男孩從水中拉起。
The boy was in bad shape but alive.	男孩狀況很不好，但是還活著。
We were all overjoyed.	我們都很高興。
Saving his life was awesome.	救了他一命，感覺很棒。
This event taught me a lesson.	這件事情給我一個教訓。
I realized how precious life is.	我了解了生命的可貴。
That was my happiest moment.	那是我的幸福時刻。

** ————————————————

fortunately〔ˋfɔrtʃənɪtlɪ〕*adv.* 幸好
good〔gʊd〕*adj.* 擅長的；熟練的   swimmer〔ˋswɪmɚ〕*n.* 游泳者
a good swimmer 游泳好手   immediately〔ɪˋmidɪɪtlɪ〕*adv.* 立即
jump〔dʒʌmp〕*v.* 跳   great〔gret〕*adj.* 大的；奮力的
struggle〔ˋstrʌgl〕*n.* 努力；奮鬥   pull〔pʊl〕*v.* 拉
in bad shape 身體狀況不好   alive〔əˋlaɪv〕*adj.* 活著的
overjoyed〔͵ovɚˋdʒɔɪd〕*adj.* 非常高興的
save〔sev〕*v.* 拯救   awesome〔ˋɔsəm〕*adj.* 極好的
event〔ɪˋvɛnt〕*n.* 事件   taught〔tɔt〕*v.* 教導（teach 的過去式）
lesson〔ˋlɛsn̩〕*n.* 教訓   realize〔ˋriə͵laɪz〕*v.* 了解
precious〔ˋprɛʃəs〕*adj.* 珍貴的

○背景說明

　　從小到大，經歷過許多事情，有快樂的、難過的、難忘的、感動的，有沒有一個經驗讓你覺得是最快樂、最幸福的時刻？本篇演講稿，要教你如何生動地描述你感到最幸福快樂的時刻。

1. *Others leave a lasing impression*.

others〔ˋʌðəz〕*pron.* 其他的人或物【some…others 有些…有些】
leave〔liv〕*v.* 留下　　lasting〔ˋlæstɪŋ〕*adj.* 長久的
impression〔ɪmˋprɛʃən〕*n.* 印象

　　這句話的意思是「有些留下長久的印象。」這裡的 others 是對應上一句的 Some things 而來，也可以寫成 other things，這是常用的句型，例如：

6

> *Some* people like to travel while *other* people
> like to stay at home.

（有些人喜歡去旅行，而有些人喜歡待在家。）

> Although *some* people enjoyed the book,
> 　　*others* thought it was terrible.

（雖然有些人喜歡這本書，有些人卻覺得很糟糕。）

travel〔ˋtrævḷ〕*v.* 旅行
while〔hwaɪl〕*conj.* 然而
enjoy〔ɪnˋdʒɔɪ〕*v.* 喜愛
thought〔ðɔt〕*v.* 認為（think 的過去式）
terrible〔ˋtɛrəbḷ〕*adj.* 糟糕的

這句話也可以說成：

Others stay with you for a long time.
（有些會伴隨著你很久。）

Other things stick with you for the rest of
　　your life.（有些事情會伴隨著你的餘生。）

stick with　緊緊跟著；伴隨
for the rest of one's life　餘生

2. *I received a perfect score on my examinations.*

receive〔rɪ'siv〕*v.* 收到　　perfect〔'pɝfɪkt〕*adj.* 完美的
score〔skor〕*n.* 分數　　***perfect score***　滿分
examination〔ɪɡ,zæmə'neʃən〕*n.* 考試（= *exam*）

　　這句的意思是「我考試得到滿分。」a perfect
score 是「滿分」的意思，為美式用法，英式用法說
成 full marks，而 top marks 則是「最高分」，例如：

She got ***full marks*** in French.
（她法文得了滿分。）

He got ***top marks*** for history.
（她歷史得了最高分。）

mark〔mɑrk〕*n.* 分數　　French〔frɛntʃ〕*n.* 法文
history〔'hɪstrɪ〕*n.* 歷史

這句話也可以說成：

I aced the examinations.（我考試得到高分。）

I got a perfect score on my tests.（我考試得滿分。）

ace〔es〕*v.* 在⋯得高分（= *receive a grade of A on*）

3. *I felt like I had won the whole world.*

   feel like 覺得好像

   won〔wʌn〕v. 贏得（win 的過去式和過去分詞）

   whole〔hol〕adj. 全部的　　world〔wɜld〕n. 世界

   這句話的意思是「我覺得我好像贏得了全世界。」這句話也可以說成：

   It was like I had hit the jackpot.

   （這就像是我中了頭獎。）

   I felt like the king of the world.

   （我感覺就如同世界之王。）

   hit the jackpot 重頭獎；贏得巨大的成功

   king〔kɪŋ〕n. 國王

   feel like 的另一個用法是：feel like + V-ing，表示「想要～」，例如：

   I *felt like* going for a walk.

   （我想要去散步。）

   It is threatening to rain. I don't *feel like* going out.

   （好像要下雨了，我不想要出門。）

   go for a walk 去散步

   threaten〔ˈθrɛtn̩〕v. 有…的徵兆；好像要

4. *The boy was in bad shape but alive.*

in bad shape 身體狀況不好　　alive〔əˋlaɪv〕*adj.* 活著的

　　這句話的意思是「男孩身體狀況很不好，但是還活著。」
in bad shape 的意思是「身體狀況不好」(= *out of shape*)；in good shape 則表示「身體狀況良好」；get
in shape 意思是「保持良好身體狀況」，例如：

Tom needs exercise. He's *in bad shape*.
（湯姆需要運動，他的身體狀況不好。）

The old actor is still *in good shape*.
（這位年老的演員身體狀況還很好。）

I must *get in shape*; otherwise, I will lose
　the game.
（我必須保持良好的身體狀況，否則我會輸了比賽。）

need〔nid〕*v.* 需要　　exercise〔ˋɛksə͵saɪz〕*n.* 運動
actor〔ˋæktə〕*n.* 演員
otherwise〔ˋʌðə͵waɪz〕*adv.* 否則
lose〔luz〕*v.* 輸掉　　game〔gem〕*n.* 比賽

alive 和另一個形容詞 living 意思相同，但是 alive
要放在名詞後，living 放在名詞後，例如：

The injured man is unconscious but still *alive*.
（受傷的男子雖然失去意識，但還活著。）

We should respect all *living* things.
（我們應該要尊重所有的生物。）

injured〔ˋɪndʒəd〕*adj.* 受傷的
unconscious〔ʌnˋkɑnʃəs〕*adj.* 無意識的
respect〔rɪˋspɛkt〕*v.* 尊敬；尊重　　*living things* 生物

He was in critical condition but at least he
　　survived the ordeal.
（他的情況很危急，但是至少他從磨難中存活下來。）

The kid was in bad shape but still breathing.
（那孩童狀況不好，但還有呼吸。）

critical〔'krɪtɪkl̩〕*adj.* 危急的
condition〔kən'dɪʃən〕*n.* 情況　　*at least* 至少
survive〔sə'vaɪv〕*v.* 從…存活下來
ordeal〔ɔr'dil〕*n.* 苦難經歷；折磨；煎熬
in bad shape 狀況不好
breathe〔brið〕*v.* 呼吸

5. ***This event taught me lesson.***
　　event〔ɪ'vɛnt〕*n.* 事件
　　taught〔tɔt〕*v.* 教導（teach 的過去式）
　　lesson〔'lɛsn̩〕*n.* 教訓

　　　　這句話的意思是「這件事情給我一個教訓。」teach
sb. a lesson 是常見的搭配，表示「給某人一個教訓」，
learn a lesson 表示「學到教訓」，例如：

That girl needs to be ***taught a lesson***.
（得給那女孩一個教訓。）

I hope you have ***learned a lesson*** from this.
（我希望你已經從這學到了教訓。）

要小心不要拼成 lessen〔'lɛsn̩〕*n.* 減輕；減弱。例如：

The noise began to ***lessen***.（噪音開始減弱。）

6

這句話也可以說成：

I learned a lot from this experience.
（我從這個經驗學到很多。）

This event really opened my eyes.
（這事件真的讓我大開眼界。）

experience〔ɪk'spɪrɪəns〕*n.* 經驗
open *one's **eyes*** 使某人大開眼界

6. ***I realized how precious life is.***
realize〔'rɪə,laɪz〕*v.* 了解
precious〔'prɛʃəs〕*adj.* 珍貴的

這句話的意思是「我了解了生命的可貴。」
how + adj./adv + S + V 是常見用法，例如：

I soon realized ***how difficult*** my job was going
to be.（我很快就會了解到我的工作會有多困難。）

I wonder ***how far*** we've walked today.
（不知道我們今天走了多遠。）

這句話也可以說成：

It occurred to me that life is fragile.
（我想到生命是脆弱的。）

One minute you're here, the next you're gone.
（一分鐘前你還在這，下一分鐘你就不見了。）

it occurs to *sb.* ***that*** 某人想到
fragile〔'frædʒəl〕*adj.* 脆弱的

My Happiest Moment

Every life has its ups and downs. *Some* things are forgotten. *Others* leave a lasting impression. Such a moment came to me last year. I received a perfect score on my examinations. It was the happiest moment of my life, *or at least* I thought it was. To celebrate, my friends and I went for a picnic. We ate, danced, *and* sang songs. It was glorious.

But the fun ended with a loud cry from the lake. We were shocked to see a small boy drowning in the water. *Fortunately*, I am a good swimmer. I jumped into the lake and pulled the boy out. He was OK, *and* we were all overjoyed. *All of a sudden*, my perfect test scores didn't seem to matter. The fact that the boy survived was more important than anything else. I realized how precious life is. *From now on* I will cherish every moment of every day.

6

● 中文翻譯

我的幸福時刻

　　人生總有高潮和低潮，有些事會被遺忘了，有些則會留下長久的印象。這樣的一刻去年發生在我身上，我考試得到滿分。這是我一生中最幸福的時刻，或者至少我是這麼認為。為了慶祝，我朋友和我一起去野餐，我們吃東西、跳舞和唱歌，實在太棒了。

　　但是我們的快樂卻因為湖裡傳來叫聲而結束。我們很震驚地看到有一位小男孩快要在水中溺死了，幸好我很會游泳，我跳進湖裡把小男孩拉上岸。他沒事，我們都感到很高興。突然間，我得滿分似乎看起來沒什麼大不了，男孩倖存下來比任何其他的事都來得重要。我了解到生命的可貴，從現在起，我會珍惜每一天的每一刻。

7. My Favorite Movie

Movies come in many different varieties.
Watching movies is entertaining.
I personally enjoy watching different kinds
  of movies.

Most of the time, I like to watch romantic movies.
I also prefer movies that teach a lesson.
My favorite movie is *Save the Last Dance*.

It has romance, music and dance.
I was impressed by Julia Stiles, who played Sarah.
She is my favorite actress.

7

---

movie (ˈmuvɪ)
different (ˈdɪfrənt)
entertaining (ˌɛntɚˈtenɪŋ)
personally (ˈpɚsn̩lɪ)
kind (kaɪnd)
romantic (roˈmæntɪk)
teach a lesson
music (ˈmjuzɪk)
dance (dæns)
play (ple)

come in
variety (vəˈraɪətɪ)

enjoy (ɪnˈdʒɔɪ)
most of the time
prefer (prɪˈfɝ)
save (sev)
romance (roˈmæns)
impress (ɪmˈprɛs)
actress (ˈæktrɪs)

Save the Last Dance is set in New York City.

It's about a girl who wants to be a ballerina.

Then her mother suddenly dies.

Sarah has to go live with her dad.

She also transfers to a new school.

She has no friends until she meets Chenille.

Chenille helps Sarah and shows her around.

She gets to know Chenille's brother,

　Derrick.

She later falls in love with him.

7

set〔sɛt〕	**New York City**
ballerina〔ˌbælə'rinə〕	suddenly〔'sʌdn̩lɪ〕
die〔daɪ〕	live〔lɪv〕
dad〔dæd〕	transfer〔træns'fɝ〕
friend〔frɛnd〕	until〔ən'tɪl〕
meet〔mit〕	help〔hɛlp〕
show sb. around	**get to V.**
know〔no〕	later〔'letɚ〕
fall in love with sb.	

Derrick teaches her how to dance hip-hop.

At last, Sarah makes it into Juilliard.

She finally achieves her dream.

It's my favorite movie because I love to dance.

I was surprised how quickly Sarah learned
  the steps.

It inspired me to give it a try.

The lesson of the movie is to be yourself.

Sometimes life is a struggle.

You must always work hard and fight for what
  you want.

7

---

teach (titʃ)

at last

Juilliard ('dʒuliɑrd)

achieve (ə'tʃiv)

because (bɪ'kɔz)

quickly ('kwɪklɪ)

step (stɛp)

give it a try

struggle ('strʌgl̩)

hard (hɑrd)

hip-hop ('hɪp‚hɑp)

make it

finally ('faɪnl̩ɪ)

dream (drim)

surprised (sə'praɪzd)

learn (lɜn)

inspire (ɪn'spaɪr)

sometimes ('sʌm‚taɪmz)

work (wɜk)

fight (faɪt)

7. *My Favorite Movie*

● 演講解說

Movies come in many different varieties.	電影有很多不同的種類。
Watching movies is entertaining.	看電影很有趣。
I personally enjoy watching different kinds of movies.	我個人喜歡看各種不同的電影。
Most of the time, I like to watch romantic movies.	大多時候，我喜歡看文藝片電影。
I also prefer movies that teach a lesson.	我也偏好有教訓的電影。
My favorite movie is *Save the Last Dance.*	我最喜歡的電影是「留下最後一支舞」。
It has romance, music and dance.	它有愛情故事、音樂和舞蹈。
I was impressed by Julia Stiles, who played Sarah.	扮演莎拉的茱莉亞・史緹爾讓我印象很深刻。
She is my favorite actress.	她是我最喜歡的女演員。

7

** ————————————————

movie〔'muvɪ〕*n.* 電影　　***come in*** 以…的型態出現；有
different〔'dɪfrənt〕*adj.* 不同的　　variety〔və'raɪətɪ〕*n.* 種類；多樣性
entertainment〔ˌɛntə'tenɪŋ〕*adj.* 令人愉快的；有趣的
personally〔'pɜsn̩lɪ〕*adv.* 個人地　　enjoy〔ɪn'dʒɔɪ〕*v.* 享受；喜歡
kind〔kaɪnd〕*n.* 種類　　***most of the time*** 大多時候
romantic〔ro'mæntɪk〕*adj.* 浪漫的；愛情的　　prefer〔prɪ'fɜ〕*v.* 比較喜歡
teach a lesson 給人教訓　　save〔sev〕*v.* 保留
dance〔dæns〕*n.* 舞蹈　*n.* 跳舞　　romance〔ro'mæns〕*n.* 愛情故事；羅曼史
music〔'mjuzɪk〕*n.* 音樂　　impress〔ɪm'prɛs〕*v.* 使印象深刻
play〔ple〕*v.* 扮演　　actress〔'æktrɪs〕*n.* 女演員

Save the Last Dance is set in New York City.	「留下最後一支舞」的場景是在紐約市。
It's about a girl who wants to be a ballerina.	這是關於一個想要成爲芭蕾舞女明星的女孩。
Then her mother suddenly dies.	然後她的母親突然過世。
Sarah has to go live with her dad.	莎拉必須去和她父親同住。
She also transfers to a new school.	她也必須轉到新的學校。
She has no friends until she meets Chenille.	直到她認識雪尼爾之前,她都沒有朋友。
Chenille helps Sarah and shows her around.	雪尼爾幫助莎拉,並帶她到處看看認識環境。
She gets to know Chenille's brother, Derrick.	她得以認識雪尼爾的哥哥,德瑞克。
She later falls in love with him.	她之後愛上他。

7

** ————————————————

set〔sɛt〕*v.* 把(場景)設於　　***New York City*** 紐約市
ballerina〔ˌbæləˈrinə〕*n.* 芭蕾舞女明星
suddenly〔ˈsʌdn̩lɪ〕*adv.* 突然地　　die〔daɪ〕*v.* 死亡
live〔lɪv〕*v.* 住　　***go live with*** 去和…住(= *go to live with* = *go and live with*)　　transfer〔trænsˈfɝ〕*v.* 轉學
friend〔frɛnd〕*n.* 朋友　　until〔ənˈtɪl〕*conj.* 直到
not…until 直到~才…　　meet〔mit〕*v.* 遇見;認識
help〔hɛlp〕*v.* 幫助　　***show sb. around*** 帶某人到處看看
get to V. 得以~;能夠~　　know〔no〕*v.* 認識
later〔ˈletɚ〕*adv.* 之後;後來　　***fall in love with sb.*** 愛上某人

Derrick teaches her how to dance hip-hop. | 德瑞克教她如何跳嘻哈舞。
At last, Sarah makes it into Juilliard. | 最後，莎拉成功進入茱莉亞音樂學院。
She finally achieves her dream. | 她最後實現她的夢想。

It's my favorite movie because I love to dance. | 這是我最喜歡的電影，因為我喜歡跳舞。
I was surprised how quickly Sarah learned the steps. | 我很訝異莎拉這麼快就學會了舞步。
It inspired me to give it a try. | 這激勵我要嘗試去跳舞。

The lesson of the movie is to be yourself. | 這部電影的教訓是告訴我們要做自己。
Sometimes life is a struggle. | 有時候，人生是一場奮鬥。
You must always work hard and fight for what you want. | 你必須一直努力並爭取你想要的東西。

7

** ————————————————

teach〔titʃ〕v. 教導　hip-hop〔'hɪpˌhɑp〕n. 嘻哈【1980年代源起於美國城市黑人青少年的一種文化】　*at last* 最後
make it 成功；辦到　*make it into* 成功進入
Juilliard〔'dʒulɪɑrd〕n. 茱莉亞音樂學院【創於1905年，位於紐約市】
finally〔'faɪnlɪ〕adv. 最後　achieve〔ə'tʃiv〕v. 達成；實現
dream〔drim〕n. 夢想　because〔bɪ'kɔz〕conj. 因為
surprised〔sə'praɪzd〕adj. 驚訝的　quickly〔'kwɪklɪ〕adv. 很快地
learn〔lɜn〕v. 學習　step〔stɛp〕n. 腳步；舞步
inspire〔ɪn'spaɪr〕v. 激勵；啟發　*give it a try* 試看看
sometimes〔'sʌmˌtaɪmz〕adv. 有時候
struggle〔'strʌgl〕n. 努力；奮鬥　work〔wɜk〕v. 工作；努力
hard〔hɑrd〕adv. 努力地　fight〔faɪt〕v. 爭取 <*for*>

背景說明

　　電影是很棒的娛樂，很多人都很喜歡看電影。電影都有一個故事，除了娛樂，還可以告訴我們許多事情，像是給我們啓發、思考。本篇演講稿，就是要說明如何介紹自己喜歡的電影。

1. *Movies come in many different varieties.*

movie〔'muvɪ〕*n.* 電影　　***come in*** 以…的型態出現；有
different〔'dɪfrənt〕*adj.* 不同的
variety〔və'raɪətɪ〕*n.* 種類；多樣性

　　這句話的意思是「電影有很多不同的種類。」come in 用於事物，表示「（某事物）有…（顏色、大小等）」，例如：

The shirt *comes in* yellow and red.
（這襯衫有黃色和紅色。）

Tents *come in* various shapes and sizes.
（帳棚有各種形狀和大小。）

shirt〔ʃɜt〕*n.* 襯衫　　tent〔tɛnt〕*n.* 帳棚
various〔'vɛrɪəs〕*adj.* 各式各樣的
shape〔ʃep〕*n.* 形狀　　size〔saɪz〕*n.* 大小；尺寸

這句話也可以說成：

There are many different types of movies.
（有許多種不同類型的電影。）

7

Films come in a wide variety of genres.

（電影有許多種類型。）

type〔 taɪp 〕n. 型式；類別
film〔 fɪlm 〕n. 電影　　wide〔 waɪd 〕adj. 廣泛的
a wide variety of 很多各式各樣的
genre〔'ʒɑnrə 〕n. （藝術、文學等）類型

2. *I personally enjoy watching different kinds of movies.*
personally〔'pɝsn̩l̩ɪ 〕adv. 個人地
enjoy〔 ɪn'dʒɔɪ 〕v. 享受；喜愛
different〔'dɪfərənt 〕adj. 不同的　　　kind〔 kaɪnd 〕n. 種類

　　　這句話的意思是：「我個人喜歡看各種不同的電影。」
personally 是 personal（個人的）的副詞，還可以用來
表示「親自；針對個人地」，例如：

He will deal with the problem *personally*.
（他會親自處理問題。）

Don't take it *personally*.（不要認為這是針對個人。）

這句話也可以說成：

Many different types of movies appeal to me.
（很多不同類型的電影都吸引我。）

I'm not loyal to any one type of film genre.
（我並沒有忠於任何一種電影類型。）

appeal to 吸引（ = *attract* ）
loyal〔'lɔɪəl 〕adj. 忠誠的 < *to* >

7

3. *Save the Last Dance is set in New York City.*

set〔sɛt〕*v.* 把（場景）設於（三態變化為 set-set-set）
New York City 紐約市

這句話的意思是「『留下最後一支舞』的場景是在紐約市。」set 常見的意思是「設立；安置」，這裡的用法是「把（戲劇、小說、電影等）的場景設立於…」，故名詞 setting〔'sɛtɪŋ〕意思為「場景」，例如：

The play that is *set* in 16th-century Venice.

（這齣戲的場景是在十六世紀的威尼斯。）

The play has its *setting* in Venice.

（這齣戲的場景是在威尼斯。）

這句話也可以說成：

Save the Last Dance takes place
　　in Manhattan.

（「留下最後的一支舞」發生在曼哈頓。）

New York City provides the backdrop
　　for *Save the Last Dance.*

（紐約市提供了「留下最後一支舞」的場景。）

take place 發生；舉行
Manhattan〔mæn'hætn̩〕*n.* 曼哈頓【紐約市的一區】
provide〔prə'vaɪd〕*v.* 提供
backdrop〔'bæk,drɑp〕*n.* 背景

7

4. **Chenille helps Sarah and shows her around.**

help〔hɛlp〕v. 幫助　　**show sb. around** 帶某人到處看看

　　這句話的意思是「雪尼爾幫助莎拉並帶她到處看看
認識環境。」show *sb.* around 是很好用的片語，意
思是「帶某人參觀；帶某人到處看看」，可以用在很多
地方，例如：

Would you ***show me around***?
（你可以帶我參觀一下嗎？）

I will get someone to ***show you around***.
（我會找人帶你到處看看。）

這句話也可以說成：

Chenille takes Sarah under her wing.
（雪尼爾照顧莎拉。）

Sarah is befriended by Chenille, who shows
　　her the ropes.
（莎拉受到雪尼爾的照顧，雪尼爾還教她訣竅。）

take sb. under one's wing 照顧某人（= *take care of sb.*）
befriend〔bɪ'frɛnd〕v. 和…交朋友；照顧
the ropes 方法；訣竅　　***show sb. the ropes*** 教某人訣竅

5. **At last, Sarah makes it into Juilliard.**

at last 最後；終於　　**make it** 成功；辦到
make it into 成功進入
Juilliard〔'dʒulɪɑrd〕n. 茱莉亞音樂學院

　　這句話的意思是「最後，莎拉成功進入茱莉亞音樂學院。」

Juilliard（茱莉亞音樂學院）是世界著名的表演藝術學校
之一，位於美國紐約市的林肯中心。學校的課程分爲舞蹈、
戲劇與音樂三個專業學科，是許多熱愛音樂的人想要進入
的學校，這也是爲何這是故事裡的主角夢寐以求的目標。

　　這句話 make it 有「成功；辦到；及時趕到；出席」
的意思；如果是 make it big 則是「大獲成功；走紅」，例如：

Eric ***made it*** in films when he was still a

　　teenager.（艾瑞克還是青少年時就在電影界成功了。）

We just ***made it*** in time for the meeting.

（我們剛好及時趕到會議。）

It is not easy to ***make it big*** in entertainment.

（要在娛樂圈走紅並不容易。）

films〔fɪlmz〕*n.*【集合稱】電影界
teenager〔'tin͵edʒɚ〕*n.* 青少年
just〔dʒʌst〕*adv.* 剛好　　***in time*** 及時
meeting〔'mitɪŋ〕*n.* 會議
entertainment〔͵ɛntɚ'tenmənt〕*n.* 娛樂

7

這句話也可以說成：

In the end, Sarah is accepted by Juilliard

（最後，莎拉被茱莉亞音樂學院接受了。）

Finally, Sarah gets into Juilliard.

（最後，莎拉進入了茱莉亞音樂學院。）

in the end 最後　　accept〔ək'sɛpt〕*v.* 接受
get into 進入；入（學）

6. *The lesson of the movie is to be yourself.*

lesson〔'lɛsn̩〕*n.* 教訓

　　　　這句話的意思是「這部電影的教訓是要做自己。」。
be *oneself* 是「做自己」的意思，也就是不要隨波逐流，
沒有自己的想法或意見，許多名人都有類似的想法，例如：

Be yourself; everyone else is already taken.
（做你自己；其他角色都已經有人了。）

To be yourself in a world that is constantly
　　trying to make you something else is the
　　greatest accomplishment.
（身處於一個不斷要讓你變成其他事物的世界裡，
　　還能做自己是最偉大的成就。）

constantly〔'kɑnstəntlɪ〕*adv.* 不斷地
else〔ɛls〕*adj.* 其他的；別的
accomplishment〔ə'kɑmplɪʃmənt〕*n.* 成就

7

　　這句話也可以說成：

The moral of the story is to be true to yourself.
（這故事的寓意是要忠於自己。）

The main idea of the story is to hold on to
　　your dreams.
（這故事的主旨是要堅持你的夢想。）

moral〔'mɔrəl〕*n.* 寓意；道德教訓　　*be true to* 忠於
main〔men〕*adj.* 主要的　　*main idea* 主旨
idea〔aɪ'diə〕*n.* 主意；想法　　*hold on to* 緊握著；堅持

● 作文範例

My Favorite Movie

Movies come in many different varieties. I prefer movies that teach a lesson and are related to life. My favorite movie is *Save the Last Dance*. It combines my three favorite things in life: romance, music and dance.

Save the Last Dance is about a girl named Sarah who wants to be a ballerina. *But after* her mother dies, Sarah has to go live with her dad in a bad neighborhood. She has trouble making friends until she meets Chenille and her brother Derrick. He teaches her how to dance hip-hop. With the help of Chenille and Derrick, Sarah revives her dream of being a ballerina. Learning the hip-hop moves actually improves her ballet skills. *At last*, Sarah makes it into Juilliard.

The lesson of the movie is to be yourself. *Sometimes* life is a struggle. You must always work hard and fight for what you want.

7

● 中文翻譯

我最喜愛的電影

電影有許多不同的類型。我偏好有教訓的並且和人生有關的電影。我最喜愛的電影是「留下最後一支舞」，這都電影結合了生命中三樣我最喜愛的東西：愛情、音樂和舞蹈。

「留下最後一支舞」是關於一位名叫莎拉的女孩，她想要成為芭蕾舞女明星。但是在她母親過世後，她必須去和她父親同住在一個不好的地方。她很難交到朋友，直到她遇到雪尼爾和她的哥哥德瑞克。德瑞克教她如何跳嘻哈舞。有雪尼爾和德瑞克的幫助，莎拉重振她成為芭蕾舞女的夢想。學習嘻哈的舞步確實也增進了她芭蕾舞的技巧。最後，莎拉成功進入了茱莉亞音樂學院。

這部電影的教訓是要我們做自己。有時候，人生是一場奮鬥，你必須一直努力並爭取你想要的東西。

8. My Favorite Subject

Some students prefer to study math.
Others prefer to study history.
It's easier to memorize things than solve a
  mathematical theory.

My favorite subject is English.
Others have tried to discourage me.
They say I am wasting my time.

Some people think English is useless.
However, I think it's interesting and fun.
I love learning different languages.

8

favorite ('fevərɪt)	subject ('sʌbdʒɪkt)
prefer (prɪ'fɝ)	study ('stʌdɪ)
math (mæθ)	history ('hɪstrɪ)
memorize ('mɛmə‚raɪz)	solve (salv)
mathematical (‚mæθə'mætɪkḷ)	
theory ('θiərɪ)	discourage (dɪs'kɝɪdʒ)
waste (west)	useless ('juslɪs)
however (haʊ'ɛvɚ)	interesting ('ɪntrɪstɪŋ)
fun (fʌn)	learn (lɝn)
different ('dɪfrənt)	language ('læŋgwɪdʒ)

I especially enjoy reading English books.

Reading in itself is a great pleasure.

English has a wealth of literature.

It gives us an insight into human nature.

We realize what actions bring what reactions.

We learn to look for deeper meaning.

In addition to reading, I like to practice my
  speaking skills.

I have several foreign friends.

We have language exchanges.

8

especially (ə'spɛʃəlɪ)   enjoy (ɪn'dʒɔɪ)
in itself   pleasure ('plɛʒɚ)
wealth (wɛlθ)   *a wealth of*
literature ('lɪtərətʃɚ)   insight ('ɪn,saɪt)
human ('hjumən)   nature ('netʃɚ)
realize ('rɪə,laɪz)   action ('ækʃən)
bring (brɪŋ)   reaction (rɪ'ækʃən)
look for   deeper ('dipɚ)
meaning ('minɪŋ)   *in addition to*
practice ('præktɪs)   skill (skɪl)
foreign ('fɔrɪn)   exchange (ɪks'tʃendʒ)

English is the international language.
It is an open door to the world.
English can take you places.

Learning English will help me in the future.
I plan to study overseas.
English is a necessity.

Studying and practicing English is never
  a chore.
Every day is a new set of challenges.
That is why English is my favorite subject.

---

international (ˌɪntɚˈnæʃənl̩)
door (dor)   ***take sb. places***
help (hɛlp)   future (ˈfjutʃɚ)
plan (plæn)   overseas (ˈovɚˈsiz)
necessity (nəˈsɛsətɪ)   chore (tʃor)
set (sɛt)   challenge (ˈtʃælɪndʒ)

8

8. *My Favorite Subject*

演講解說

Some students prefer to study math.	有些人偏好讀數學。
Others prefer to study history.	有些人偏好讀歷史。
It's easier to memorize things than	記憶東西比起解數學理論來
solve a mathematical theory.	得簡單。
My favorite subject is English.	我最喜愛的科目是英文。
Others have tried to discourage me.	其他人試著要勸阻我。
They say I am wasting my time.	他們說我是在浪費時間。
Some people think English is useless.	有些人覺得英文沒有用。
However, I think it's interesting	然而,我覺得英文有趣又好
and fun.	玩。
I love learning different languages.	我喜歡學不同的語言。

8

** —————————————————————————

favorite〔'fevərɪt〕adj. 最喜愛的　　subject〔'sʌbdʒɪkt〕n. 科目
prefer〔prɪ'fɜ〕v. 較喜歡;偏好　　study〔'stʌdɪ〕v. 研讀
math〔mæθ〕n. 數學　　history〔'hɪstrɪ〕n. 歷史
memorize〔'mɛmə,raɪz〕v. 背誦;記憶　　solve〔salv〕v. 解決
mathematical〔,mæθə'mætɪkḷ〕adj. 數學的　　theory〔'θɪərɪ〕n. 理論
discourage〔dɪs'kɝɪdʒ〕v. 反對;勸阻　　waste〔west〕v. 浪費
useless〔'juslɪs〕adj. 沒用的　　however〔haʊ'ɛvɚ〕adv. 然而
interesting〔'ɪntrɪstɪŋ〕adj. 有趣的　　fun〔fʌn〕adj. 有趣的;好玩的
learn〔lɝn〕v. 學習　　different〔'dɪfrənt〕adj. 不同的
language〔'læŋgwɪdʒ〕n. 語言

I especially enjoy reading English books.	我特別喜歡讀英文書。
Reading in itself is a great pleasure.	閱讀本身是個很愉快的事。
English has a wealth of literature.	英文有豐富的文學。
It gives us an insight into human nature.	它讓我們我洞悉人性。
We realize what actions bring what reactions.	我們了解的怎樣的行為會帶來怎樣的結果。
We learn to look for deeper meaning.	我們學著去尋找更深的意義。
In addition to reading, I like to practice my speaking skills.	除了閱讀，我還喜歡練習我的說話技巧。
I have several foreign friends.	我有好幾個外國朋友。
We have language exchanges.	我們有語言交換。

**

especially〔ə'spɛʃəlɪ〕*adv.* 尤其；特別地

enjoy〔ɪn'dʒɔɪ〕*v.* 享受；喜愛　　read〔rid〕*v.* 閱讀

in itself 本身；本質上　　pleasure〔'plɛʒɚ〕*n.* 愉快的事

wealth〔wɛlθ〕*n.* 豐富　　*a wealth of* 豐富的

literature〔'lɪtərətʃɚ〕*n.* 文學　　insight〔'ɪn,saɪt〕*n.* 洞察力；眼光

human〔'hjumən〕*adj.* 人的　　nature〔'netʃɚ〕*n.* 天性；本質

realize〔'riə,laɪz〕*v.* 了解　　action〔'ækʃən〕*n.* 行為

bring〔brɪŋ〕*v.* 帶來　　reaction〔rɪ'ækʃən〕*n.* 反應；結果

look for 尋找　　deeper〔'dipɚ〕*adj.* 更深的

meaning〔'minɪŋ〕*n.* 意義　　*in addition to* 除了…（還有）

practice〔'præktɪs〕*v.* 練習　　skill〔skɪl〕*n.* 技巧；技能

foreign〔'fɔrɪn〕*adj.* 外國的　　exchange〔ɪks'tʃendʒ〕*n.* 交換

8

English is the international language.	英文是國際的語言。
It is an open door to the world.	它是通往世界的門。
English can take you places.	英文可以帶你到各地。
Learning English will help me in the future.	學英文在未來對我會有幫助。
I plan to study overseas.	我計畫出國讀書。
English is a necessity.	英文是必要的。
Studying and practicing English is never a chore.	研讀和練習英文從來都不是件無聊的事。
Every day is a new set of challenges.	每一天都是要面對一系列新的挑戰。
That is why English is my favorite subject.	那就是為什麼英文是我最喜愛的科目。

8

** ————————————————

international〔͵ɪntɚˋnæʃənḷ〕*adj.* 國際的
door〔dor〕*n.* 門；道路　　***take sb. places*** 帶某人到各地
help〔hɛlp〕*v.* 幫助　　future〔ˋfjutʃɚ〕*n.* 未來
plan〔plæn〕*v.* 計畫；打算　　overseas〔ˋovɚˋsiz〕*adv.* 在國外
necessity〔nəˋsɛsətɪ〕*n.* 必要
chore〔tʃor〕*n.* 無聊的事；雜務
set〔sɛt〕*n.* 一套；一系列　　challenge〔ˋtʃælɪndʒ〕*n.* 挑戰

背景說明

　　從國小、國中甚至到高中，我們都學了很多科目，從學科到術科，不勝枚舉。接觸這麼多的科目，有沒有哪一個觸發了你的興趣呢？讓你願意孜孜不倦地學習？本篇演講稿，讓你有機會說說你最愛的科目。

1. *It's easier to memorize things than solve a mathematical theory.*

memorize〔'mɛmə,raɪz〕v. 背誦；記憶
solve〔sɑlv〕v. 解決；解釋
mathematical〔,mæθə'mætɪkl̩〕adj. 數學的
theory〔'θiərɪ〕n. 理論

　　這句話的意思是「記憶東西比起解釋數學理論來得簡單。」memorize（背誦；記憶）的名詞是 memory〔'mɛmərɪ〕n. 記憶，例如：

The boy can *memorize* the data easily.
（那小男孩可以輕易地記住這些資料。）

If my *memory* serves me, he was the thief.
（如果我沒記錯，他就是那個小偷。）

data〔'detə〕n. pl. 資料　　easily〔'izəlɪ〕adv. 輕易地
if memory serves (*sb. right*)　如果某人沒記錯的話
thief〔θif〕n. 小偷

8

這句話也可以說成：

Memorization takes less effort than solving
a math equation.

（比起解數學方程式，記憶較不費力。）

Math is more difficult than memorizing
words. （數學比記憶詞彙難。）

memorization〔͵mɛmərə'zeʃən〕n. 記憶；背誦
take〔tek〕v. 花費　　effort〔'ɛfət〕n. 努力
equation〔ɪ'kweʒən〕n. 方程式
word〔wɝd〕n. 單字；詞彙

2. *Others have tried to discourage me*.
try〔traɪ〕v. 嘗試
discourage〔dɪs'kɝɪdʒ〕v. 反對；勸阻

這句話的意思是「其他人試著要勸阻我。」
discourage 的常用句型是：discourage *sb*. from
V-ing（打消某人做…的念頭；阻止某人做…）：

The bad weather *discouraged us from*
climbing the mountain.

（壞天氣讓我們打消去爬山的念頭。）

They tried to *discourage their son from*
marrying the girl.

（他們試著要阻止兒子和那女子結婚。）

【marry〔'mærɪ〕v. 和…結婚】

這句話也可以說成：

People tell me I'm crazy. (大家都說我瘋了。)

My friends have not been supportive.
(我的朋友並不支持我。)

crazy〔'krezɪ〕adj. 發瘋的
supportive〔sə'portɪv〕adj. 支持的

3. *Reading in itself is a great pleasure.*

in itself 本身；本質上
pleasure〔'plɛʒɚ〕n. 樂趣；愉快的事

　　這句話的意思是「閱讀本身就是件很愉快的事。」in itself 是「本身；本質上」的意思，也可以寫成 of itself，要注意，這個詞彙因為是 itself，所以要用於「事物」身上，如果用在「人或動物」，要用 by nature (生性；天生地)，例如：

Stress *in itself* is not necessarily injurious.
(壓力本身不一定有害。)

Using someone else's name is not *of itself*
　a crime, unless there is an intention to
　to commit a fraud.
(使用他人的名字本身不是犯罪，除非有詐騙動機。)

She is quiet and shy *by nature*. (她天性安靜又害羞。)

stress〔strɛs〕n. 壓力　　*not necessarily* 未必；不一定
injurious〔ɪn'dʒʊrɪəs〕adj. 有害的
crime〔kraɪm〕n. 罪

8

intention〔ɪn'tɛnʃən〕n. 意圖；動機
commit〔kə'mɪt〕v. 犯（罪）　　fraud〔frɔd〕n. 詐欺
quiet〔'kwaɪət〕adj. 安靜的　　shy〔ʃaɪ〕adj. 害羞的

這句話也可以説成：

There is a good deal of pleasure in reading.
（閱讀是非常愉快的事。）

Reading is a worthwhile activity.
（閱讀是個值得的活動。）

a good deal of 很多的
worthwhile〔'wɝθ'hwaɪl〕adj. 值得的；值得花時間的
activity〔æk'tɪvətɪ〕n. 活動

4. ***It gives us an insight into human nature.***
insight〔'ɪn,saɪt〕n. 洞察力；眼光
human〔'hjumən〕adj. 人的
nature〔'netʃɚ〕n. 天性；本質

這句話的意思是「它讓我們洞悉人性。」insight
常和 into 連用；of insight 放在名詞後，表示「有洞
察力的」（= *insightful*），例如：

Good teachers have ***insight into*** the problems
of students.
（好老師可以洞察學生的問題。）

He is a writer ***of great insight***.
（他是個很有洞察力的作家。）

【insightful〔ɪn'saɪtfəl〕adj. 有洞察力的】

5. ***We realize what actions bring what reactions***.

realize〔'riə,laɪz〕*v.* 了解　　action〔'ækʃən〕*n.* 動作
bring〔brɪŋ〕*v.* 帶來　　reaction〔rɪ'ækʃən〕*n.* 反應

　　　　這句話的字面意思是「我們了解怎樣的行為會帶
來怎樣的反應。」意思其實是「我們了解怎樣的行為
會有怎麼樣的後果。」也可以說成：

We see the causes and the effects.
（我們看到了原因和結果。）

We understand the consequences of our deeds.
（我們了解我們行為的後果。）

cause〔kɔz〕*n.* 原因　　effect〔ɪ'fɛkt〕*n.* 效果；結果
consequence〔'kɑnsə,kwɛns〕*n.* 後果
deed〔did〕*n.* 行為

6. ***It is an open door to the world***.

open〔'opən〕*adj.* 打開的　　door〔dor〕*n.* 門；道路

　　　　這句話的字面意思是「它是通往世界的門。」door
除了「門」，可以引申為「通道；途徑」，和介系詞 to
連用，例如：

The ***door to*** knowledge is study.
（通往知識的道路是學習。）

Diligence is the ***door to*** success.
（勤勉是通往成功的途徑。）

knowledge〔'nɑlɪdʒ〕*n.* 知識　　study〔'stʌdɪ〕*n.* 讀書
diligence〔'dɪlədʒəns〕*n.* 勤勉
success〔sək'sɛs〕*n.* 成功

8

這句話也可以說成：

It is the key to the world.（它是打開世界的鑰匙。）

It is the gateway to the world.
（它是通往世界的入口。）

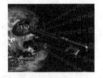

key〔ki〕*n.* 鑰匙；關鍵 < *to* >
gateway〔'get‚we〕*n.* 入口；途徑 < *to* >

7. *English can take you places.*

take sb. places 帶某人到各地

這句話的意思是「英文可以帶你到各地。」take *sb.*
places 字面意思是「帶某人到各地」，可引申為「促進
某人的事業或成功」(= *advance somebody's career
or success*)，例如：

Let travel *take you places.*
（讓旅行帶你到各地去吧。）

Confidence can *take you places.*
（自信對你的成功有幫助。）

advance〔əd'væns〕*v.* 促進
career〔kə'rɪr〕*n.* 事業　　travel〔'trævl̩〕*n.* 旅行
confidence〔'kɑnfədəns〕*n.* 自信

這句話也可以說成：

English can take you where you want to go.
（英文可以帶你到你想去的地方。）

English can take you places you never dreamed
　possible.（英文可帶你到你沒想過可能去的地方。）

作文範例

My Favorite Subject

Every student has a favorite subject. My favorite subject, English, is rather uncommon among my peers. My friends and family have tried to discourage me. They say I am wasting my time, *but* I don't agree.

There are several things I like about English. I especially enjoy reading English books. Reading in itself is a great pleasure, *and* there is a wealth of literature in English. Reading gives us an insight into human nature. We realize what actions bring what reactions. We learn to look for deeper meaning. *In addition to* reading, I like to practice my speaking skills. I have several foreign friends and we have language exchanges. English is the international language. It is an open door to the world. I plan to study overseas, *so* English is a necessity.

Studying and practicing English is never a chore. Every day is a new set of challenges. That is why English is my favorite subject.

8

我最喜愛的科目

　　每個學生都有最喜愛的科目，我最喜愛的科目是英文，這在我的同儕中是相當罕見的。我朋友和家人嘗試著要勸阻我。他們說我是在浪費時間，但我不同意。

　　關於英文，有一些東西是我喜歡的。我特別喜歡閱讀英文書籍，讀書本身就是件很愉快的事，而且英文裡有豐富的文學。閱讀讓我們洞悉人性，我們了解到什麼行為會有怎樣的後果，並學著尋找更深層的意義。除了閱讀，我還喜歡練習我的說話技巧。我有好幾個外國朋友，並且彼此有語言交換。英文是國際語言，它是通往世界的門。我計畫要出國讀書，所以英文是必要的。

　　研讀和練習英文從來都不會無聊，每一天都是一系列新的挑戰，那就是為何英文會是我最喜愛的科目。

9. My Dream

I am a lucky person.
I am lucky because I know what I want.
I have always had a direction in life.

I have many hopes and ambitions for the future.
However, there is one thing I want most.
I want to be a buyer for a clothing company.

I have been interested in fashion my whole life.
I love to go shopping for clothes.
I read all the fashion magazines.

dream〔drim〕
because〔bɪˈkɔz〕
hope〔hop〕
future〔ˈfjutʃɚ〕
buyer〔ˈbaɪɚ〕
company〔ˈkʌmpənɪ〕
fashion〔ˈfæʃən〕
go shopping
magazine〔ˈmægəˌzin〕

lucky〔ˈlʌkɪ〕
direction〔dəˈrɛkʃən〕
ambition〔æmˈbɪʃən〕
however〔haʊˈɛvɚ〕
clothing〔ˈkloðɪŋ〕
interested〔ˈɪntrɪstɪd〕
whole〔hol〕
clothes〔kloz〕

9

***So far*, *I have taken steps toward my goal*.**
My formal education is the starting point.
I believe that it will continue to be an asset.

My first and foremost plan is to graduate
　from high school.
I consider this to be a huge accomplishment.
After graduation, I will go to college.

In college, I will study business and fashion.
I will dedicate myself to realizing my dream.
I will obtain the knowledge I need.

---

so far
toward ﹝ tord ﹞
formal ﹝'fɔrml̩ ﹞
starting point
continue ﹝ kən'tɪnju ﹞
first and foremost
graduate ﹝'grædʒu,et ﹞
consider ﹝ kən'sɪdə ﹞
accomplishment ﹝ ə'kamplɪʃmənt ﹞
graduation ﹝,grædʒu'eʃən ﹞
business ﹝'bɪznɪs ﹞
realize ﹝'rɪə,laɪz ﹞
knowledge ﹝'nɑlɪdʒ ﹞

step ﹝ stɛp ﹞
goal ﹝ gol ﹞
education ﹝,ɛdʒə'keʃən ﹞
believe ﹝ bɪ'liv ﹞
asset ﹝'æsɛt ﹞
plan ﹝ plæn ﹞
high school
huge ﹝ hjudʒ ﹞
college ﹝'kɑlɪdʒ ﹞
dedicate ﹝'dɛdə,ket ﹞
obtain ﹝ əb'ten ﹞
need ﹝ nid ﹞

What happens after that is hard to say.
My education will be my foundation.
However, the world changes so quickly.

I must remain flexible.
As I get older, I will see things differently.
Perhaps my dream will change.

The most important thing is to stay
   focused.
Now I work toward making it real.
I will succeed in anything I choose to do.

happen (ˈhæpən)	***be hard to say***
foundation (faʊnˈdeʃən)	change (tʃendʒ)
quickly (ˈkwɪklɪ)	remain (rɪˈmen)
flexible (ˈflɛksəbl)	get (gɛt)
differently (ˈdɪfrəntlɪ)	perhaps (pəˈhæps)
important (ɪmˈpɔrtn̩t)	stay (ste)
focused (ˈfokəst)	***work toward***
make sth. ***real***	succeed (səkˈsid)
choose (tʃuz)	

9

9. *My Dream*

● 演講解說

I am a lucky person.	我是個幸運的人。
I am lucky because I know what I want.	我很幸運，因為我知道我想要什麼。
I have always had a direction in life.	我總是有一個人生的方向。
I have many hopes and ambitions for the future.	我未來有很多希望和志向。
However, there is one thing I want most.	然而，有一樣東西是我最想要的。
I want to be a buyer for a clothing company.	我想要成為一家服裝公司的採購。
I have been interested in fashion my whole life.	我一生都對時尚很感興趣。
I love to go shopping for clothes.	我喜歡去購物買衣服。
I read all the fashion magazines.	所有的時尚雜誌我都讀。

9

** ——————————————

dream〔drim〕*n.* 夢想　　lucky〔'lʌkɪ〕*adj.* 幸運的

because〔bɪ'kɔz〕*conj.* 因為　　direction〔də'rɛkʃən〕*n.* 方向

hope〔hop〕*n.* 希望　　ambition〔æm'bɪʃən〕*n.* 志向；野心；抱負

however〔haʊ'ɛvɚ〕*adv.* 然而　　buyer〔'baɪɚ〕*n.* 購買者；採購員

clothing〔'kloðɪŋ〕*n.* 【集合名詞】衣服　　company〔'kʌmpənɪ〕*n.* 公司

interested〔'ɪntrɪstɪd〕*adj.* 感興趣的 < in >

fashion〔'fæʃən〕*n.* 時尚；時裝　　whole〔hol〕*adj.* 全部的

go shopping 去購物　　clothes〔kloz〕*n. pl.* 衣服

magazine〔'mægə,zin〕*n.* 雜誌

So far, *I have taken steps toward my goal*.　到目前為止，為了我的目標，我已經採取一些步驟。

My formal education is the starting point.　我的正規教育是起點。

I believe that it will continue to be an asset.　我相信這將會持續是我的資產。

My first and foremost plan is to graduate from high school.　我的首要計畫是要從高中畢業。

I consider this to be a huge accomplishment.　我認為這是很大的成就。

After graduation, I will go to college.　畢業後，我要上大學。

In college, I will study business and fashion.　唸大學時，我會研讀商學和時尚。

I will dedicate myself to realizing my dream.　我會致力於實現我的夢想。

I will obtain the knowledge I need.　我會獲得我需要的知識。

** ———————————————————

so far 到目前為止　　step〔stɛp〕*n.* 步驟
toward〔tord〕*prep.* 朝向；為了　　goal〔gol〕*n.* 目標
formal〔'fɔrml̩〕*adj.* 正式的；正規的　　education〔,ɛdʒə'keʃən〕*n.* 教育
starting point 起點　　believe〔bɪ'liv〕*v.* 相信
continue〔kən'tɪnju〕*v.* 持續　　asset〔'æsɛt〕*n.* 資產；有用的東西
first and foremost 首要的　　plan〔plæn〕*v.* 計畫；打算
graduate〔'grædʒu,et〕*v.* 畢業　　*high school* 高中
consider〔kən'sɪdɚ〕*v.* 認為　　huge〔hjudʒ〕*adj.* 巨大的
accomplishment〔ə'kamplɪʃmənt〕*n.* 成就
graduation〔,grædʒu'eʃən〕*n.* 畢業　　college〔'kalɪdʒ〕*n.* 大學
business〔'bɪznɪs〕*n.* 商業　　dedicate〔'dɛdə,ket〕*v.* 使致力於
dedicate oneself to 致力於　　realize〔'rɪə,laɪz〕*v.* 實現
obtain〔əb'ten〕*v.* 獲得　　knowledge〔'nalɪdʒ〕*n.* 知識
need〔nid〕*v.* 需要

9

What happens after that is hard to say.	往後發生的事很難說。
My education will be my foundation.	我的教育是基礎。
However, the world changes so quickly.	然而，世界變得很快。
I must remain flexible.	我必須懂得變通。
As I get older, I will see things differently.	隨著我年紀增長，我看事物的角度會不同。
Perhaps my dream will change.	或許我的夢想會改變。
The most important thing is to stay focused.	最重要的，就是要保持專注。
Now I work toward making it real.	現在我努力要讓夢想成眞。
I will succeed in anything I choose to do.	我選擇做的事情都會成功。

** —————————————————————

happen〔'hæpən〕v. 發生
be hard to say 很難說　　foundation〔faʊn'deʃən〕n. 基礎
however〔haʊ'ɛvə〕adv. 然而　　change〔tʃendʒ〕v. 改變
quickly〔'kwɪklɪ〕adv. 快速地　　remain〔rɪ'men〕v. 保持
flexible〔'flɛksəbḷ〕adj. 有彈性的；可變通的；靈活的
get〔gɛt〕v. 變得　　differently〔'dɪfrəntlɪ〕adv. 不同地
perhaps〔pə'hæps〕adv. 或許
important〔ɪm'pɔrtn̩t〕adj. 重要的
stay〔ste〕v. 保持　　focused〔'fokəst〕adj. 專注的
work toward 爲…而努力　　***make sth. real*** 使某事成眞
succeed〔sək'sid〕v. 成功 < in >　　choose〔tʃuz〕v. 選擇

● 背景說明

　　小時候，大人或長輩常常會問我們有什麼夢想，想成為怎樣的人，或是從事怎樣的工作。你有什麼夢想呢？夢想除了想像，還需要付出努力執行，才能成真。本篇演講稿，讓你有機會訴說自己的夢想，和如何付諸實行。

1. *I have always had a direction in life*.

direction 〔dəˈrɛkʃən〕 *n.* 方向

　　這句話的意思是「我總是有一個人生的方向。」人生需要有方向，才不會隨波逐流，人云亦云，direction 除了用在地理方位上，也可以引申表示抽象意義，複數則是「指引；說明」。例如：

　　The birds flew away in all *directions*.
　　（鳥向四面八方飛走。）

　　You have to follow the doctor's *directions*.
　　（你必須遵照醫生的指示。）

flew 〔flu〕 *v.* 飛（fly 的過去式）
in all directions 向四面八方（= *in every direction*）
follow 〔ˈfɑlo〕 *v.* 遵從　　doctor 〔ˈdɑktɚ〕 *n.* 醫生

這句話也可以說成：

　　I've always had goals in life.
　　（我的人生總是有目標。）

9

My life has always been lived with a purpose.
(我的人生總是過得有目標。)

goal〔gol〕*n.* 目標
live one's life 過生活   purpose〔'pɝpəs〕*n.* 目的；目標

2. *So far, I have taken steps toward my goal.*
so far 到目前爲止   step〔stɛp〕*n.* 腳步；步驟
toward〔tord〕*prep.* 朝向；爲了

　　這句話的意思是「到目前爲止，爲了我的目標，我已經採取一些步驟。」so far (到目前爲止)，常和「現在完成式」連用，也可以寫成 thus far。例如：

So far, so good. (目前爲止，一切都好。)

Thus far, I haven't heard from her.
(到目前爲止，我還沒收到她的來信。)

So far, *so good.* 目前爲止，一切都好。
hear from sb. 收到某人的來信

take steps 字面上是「走幾步路」，也可以有「採取步驟」的意思；steps 引申表示「措施」(= *measures*)，例如：

I *took a step* toward the cat. (我朝向那隻貓走了一步)

She is not content with her present life and wishes to *take steps* to improve it.
(她並不滿意目前的生活，並且希望採取措施改善。)

measures〔'mɛʒɚz〕*n. pl.* 措施
content〔kən'tɛnt〕*adj.* 滿意的 < *with* >
present〔'prɛznt〕*adj.* 目前的
life〔laɪf〕*n.* 生活   improve〔ɪm'pruv〕*v.* 改善

9

這句話也可以説成：

At this point, I have made some progress
　　toward my goal.

（這時候，我已經往我的目標有了一些進步。）

Up until now, I have only made slight
　　advancements toward my dream.

（直到現在，我已經往我的夢想更近了一步。）

at this point 在這時候
progress〔'prɑgrɛs〕*n.* 前進；進步
make progress 進步　　*up until now* 直到現在
slight〔slaɪt〕*adj.* 些許的；細微的
advancement〔əd'vænsmənt〕*n.* 進步；進展

3. *I believe that it will continue to be an asset.*
believe〔bɪ'liv〕*v.* 相信　　continue〔kən'tɪnju〕*v.* 繼續
asset〔'æsɛt〕*n.* 資產；有用的東西

　　　這句話的意思是「我相信這將會持續是我的資產。」
這裡的 asset 為引申意，原意為具體的「資產；財產」。
例如：

The business has *assets* totaling 6 million
　　pounds.（該企業資產總值達六百萬英鎊。）
Youth is a great *asset* in this job.

（這份工作，年輕是很有優勢的。）

business〔'bɪznɪs〕*n.* 公司；企業
total〔'totl̩〕*v.* 總計達　　pound〔paʊnd〕*n.* 英鎊
youth〔juθ〕*n.* 年輕　　job〔dʒɑb〕*n.* 工作

9

這句話也可以說成：

It will form a solid foundation.

（這將會形成很紮實的基礎。）

It will serve me well in later life.

（這對我往後的人生很有幫助。）

form〔fɔrm〕v. 形成
solid〔'sɑlɪd〕adj. 堅固的；紮實的
foundation〔faʊn'deʃən〕n. 基礎；根基
serve sb. well 對某人有幫助   later〔'letə〕adj. 之後的

4. *I will dedicate myself to realizing my dream*.

dedicate〔'dɛdə,ket〕v. 使致力於
dedicate oneself to V-ing 致力於…
realize〔'riə,laɪz〕v. 實現   dream〔drim〕n. 夢想

這句話的意思是「我會致力於實現我的夢想。」
dedicate *oneself* to + V-ing / N.是固定的用法，也
可以寫成 devote / commit *oneself* to，例如：

He *devoted himself to writing*.

（他致力於寫作。）

Mary *committed herself to teaching* children.

（瑪麗致力於教導孩童。）

這句話也可以說成：

I will put nothing above achieving my goal.

（我不會認為有其他事情比達到我的目標重要。）

Nothing will stand in my way.

（沒有事情可以阻擋我。）

above〔əˈbʌv〕*prep.* 在…之上；優於；勝過
in one's way 擋住某人的路；妨礙某人

5. ***What happens after is hard to say.***

happen〔ˈhæpən〕*v.* 發生
be hard to say 很難說

　　這句話的意思是「往後發生的事很難說。」
也可以說成：

There is no telling what will happen next.

（無法預測接下來會發生什麼事。）

The future is a blank canvas.

（未來是一片空白的畫布。）

There is no + V-ing 不可能～；無法～（= *It is impossible
to V.*）　　blank〔blæŋk〕*adj.* 空白的
canvas〔ˈkænvəs〕*n.* 帆布；畫布

9

6. ***I must remain flexible.***

remain〔rɪˈmen〕*v.* 保持
flexible〔ˈflɛksəbḷ〕*adj.* 有彈性的；可變通的；靈活的

　　這句話的意思是「我必須懂得變通。」flexible
原意為「有彈性的；易彎曲的」，引申意為「可變通的；
靈活的」。例如：

Copper wire is *flexible*.

（銅絲易彎曲。）

Employees like *flexible* working hours.

（員工喜歡彈性的上班時間。）

copper〔'kɑpɚ〕*n.* 銅
wire〔waɪr〕*n.* 鐵線；鐵絲
employee〔ˌɛmplɔɪ'i〕*n.* 員工
working hours 上班時間

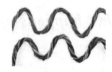

這句話也可以說成：

I must be willing to adapt.

（我必須願意去適應。）

I must be able to change course.

（我必須能夠改變方向。）

willing〔'wɪlɪŋ〕*adj.* 願意的
be willing to V. 願意～
adapt〔ə'dæpt〕*v.* 適應
be able to V. 能夠～
change〔tʃendʒ〕*v.* 改變
course〔kors〕*n.* 路線；方向
change course 改變方向

9

○ 作文範例

My Dream

A lot of my peers don't have any idea what they want to do with their lives. I am a lucky person *because* I know what I want. There is one thing I want to be more than anything else. My dream is to be a buyer for a major clothing company. Buyers go around to different designers and decide which items the company will sell. It's a very exciting job.

There are some steps I must take to reach my goal. My formal education will be the basis for my success. *Therefore*, my first step is to graduate from high school. *After* graduation I will go to college and study business and fashion. I will obtain the knowledge I need. What happens after that is hard to say. The world changes quickly, *so* I must remain flexible. The most important thing is to stay focused. *That way*, I will succeed in anything I choose to do.

9

◉中文翻譯

我的夢想

我的很多同儕對於要如何處理他的人生，沒有什麼想法。我是個幸運的人，因為我知道我要什麼。我有一件最想要做的事。我的夢想是要成為一家一流服飾公司的採購。採購要到處拜訪不同的設計師，並決定公司要賣什麼東西。這是一個很刺激的工作。

我必須採取一些步驟，來達到我的目標。我的正規教育是我成功的基礎，因此，我的第一步是要從高中畢業。畢業後，我要上大學，並研讀商學和時尚。我會獲得我需要的知識。接下來發生的事情很難說，世界改變得很快，所以我必須懂得變通。最重要的是要保持專注，那樣的話，我選擇要做的事都會成功。

9

10. A Graduation Speech

Faculty and students.
Family and friends.
It is my honor to be here.

Today is a day to be thankful.
Today is a day to be inspired.
We are all entering a new stage of life.

We have received a great education.
We are prepared to face challenges.
We have been given a priceless gift.

---

graduation 〔͵grædʒʊ'eʃən 〕
faculty 〔'fækḷtɪ 〕　　　family 〔'fæməlɪ 〕
honor 〔'ɑnə 〕　　　　thankful 〔'θæŋkfəl 〕
inspire 〔 ɪn'spaɪr 〕　　enter 〔'ɛntə 〕
stage 〔 stedʒ 〕　　　　receive 〔 rɪ'siv 〕
great 〔 gret 〕
education 〔͵ɛdʒʊ'keʃən 〕　prepare 〔 prɪ'pɛr 〕
face 〔 fes 〕　　　　　challenge 〔'tʃælɪndʒ 〕
priceless 〔'praɪslɪs 〕　gift 〔 gɪft 〕

10

***This cannot be said for all schools*.**
Here we have had a high degree of academic
　　excellence.
Whatever you decide to do next, you will
　　benefit from what you learned here.

We can also be thankful for our families.
These past three years included ups and downs.
We had our families supporting us along the way.

Finally, we can be thankful for each other.
The friendships that we have made here will
　　last a lifetime.
I hope we will continue to be there for each
　　other.

---

degree〔dɪˈgri〕
excellence〔ˈɛkslˌəns〕
next〔nɛkst〕
past〔pæst〕
ups and downs
along the way
each other
last〔læst〕
hope〔hop〕
***be there for sb*.**

academic〔ˌækəˈdɛmɪk〕
whatever〔hwɑtˈɛvɚ〕
benefit〔ˈbɛnəfɪt〕
include〔ɪnˈklud〕
support〔səˈport〕
finally〔ˈfaɪnlˌɪ〕
friendship〔ˈfrɛndˌʃɪp〕
lifetime〔ˈlaɪfˌtaɪm〕
continue〔kənˈtɪnju〕

10

Now, ***what can we be inspired by today?***
I am inspired by you—my classmates.
You have had such a great attitude in
    the face of so many setbacks.

Often on graduation day we look
    for heroes.
I see them right here among us.
We don't have to look far for inspiration.

We each have the potential to do great
    things.
Celebrate what you have accomplished.
Look forward to what you have yet to
    achieve.

---

attitude (ˈætəˌtjud)   ***in the face of***
setback (ˈsɛtˌbæk)   ***look for***
hero (ˈhɪro)   ***right here***
among (əˈmʌŋ)
inspiration (ˌɪnspəˈreʃən)   potential (pəˈtɛnʃəl)
celebrate (ˈsɛləˌbret)
accomplish (əˈkɑmplɪʃ)   ***look forward to***
have yet to V.   achieve (əˈtʃiv)

10. *A Graduation Speech*

演講解說

Faculty and students.	各位老師，各位同學。
Family and friends.	所有家人朋友們。
It is my honor to be here.	很榮幸能來到這裡。
Today is a day to be thankful.	今天是要感謝的日子。
Today is a day to be inspired.	今天是受到鼓舞的日子。
We are all entering a new stage of life.	我們都要進入一個新的人生階段。
We have received a great education.	我們經接受了很棒的教育。
We are prepared to face challenges.	我們準備好要面對挑戰。
We have been given a priceless gift.	我們都獲得了一個無價的禮物。

** ────────────────

graduation〔ˌgrædʒʊˈeʃən〕*n.* 畢業
faculty〔ˈfæklˌtɪ〕*n.* 全體教職員
family〔ˈfæməlɪ〕*n.* 家人；親人   honor〔ˈɑnɚ〕*n.* 榮幸
thankful〔ˈθæŋkfəl〕*adj.* 感謝的   inspire〔ɪnˈspaɪr〕*v.* 激勵；鼓勵
enter〔ˈɛntɚ〕*v.* 進入   stage〔stedʒ〕*n.* 階段；舞台
receive〔rɪˈsiv〕*n.* 接受   great〔gret〕*adj.* 很棒的
education〔ˌɛdʒʊˈkeʃən〕*n.* 教育   prepare〔prɪˈpɛr〕*v.* 使做好準備
face〔fes〕*v.* 面對   challenge〔ˈtʃælɪndʒ〕*n.* 挑戰
priceless〔ˈpraɪslɪs〕*adj.* 無價的   gift〔gɪft〕*n.* 禮物

This cannot be said for all schools.	並非所有學校都能這麼說。
Here we have had a high degree of academic excellence.	在這裡我們已經有了高程度的學業表現。
Whatever you decide to do next, you will benefit from what you learned here.	無論你接下來決定做什麼，你在這裡學到的東西都會對你有益。
We can also be thankful for our families.	我們要很感謝我們的家人。
These past three years included ups and downs.	這過去的三年包含了所有起伏。
We had our families supporting us along the way.	一路上有家人支持著我們。
Finally, we can be thankful for each other.	最後，我們也要感謝彼此。
The friendships that we have made here will last a lifetime.	我們在這裡的建立的友誼將會持續終生。
I hope we will continue to be there for each other.	我希望我們會一直準備好要幫助彼此。

**

degree〔dɪˋgri〕*n.* 程度　　academic〔͵ækəˋdɛmɪk〕*adj.* 學業上的
whatever〔hwɑtˋɛvɚ〕*conj.* 無論什麼
excellence〔ˋɛksləns〕*n.* 優異　　benefit〔ˋbɛnəfɪt〕*v.* 受益
thankful〔ˋθæŋkfəl〕*adj.* 感謝的　　include〔ɪnˋklud〕*v.* 包含
ups and downs 起伏；興衰　　support〔səˋport〕*v.* 支持
along the way 一路上；沿途　　finally〔ˋfaɪn̩ḷɪ〕*adv.* 最後
each other 彼此　　friendship〔ˋfrɛnd͵ʃɪp〕*n.* 友誼
last〔læst〕*v.* 持續　　lifetime〔ˋlaɪf͵taɪm〕*n.* 一生；終生
hope〔hop〕*v.* 希望　　continue〔kənˋtɪnju〕*v.* 持續
be there for *sb.* 隨叫隨到；不離開…左右；準備幫助某人

10

Now, what can we be inspired by today?

現在，我們今天可以受到什麼啓發？

I am inspired by you—my classmates.

我受到你們的啓發——我的同班同學。

You have had such a great attitude in the face of so many setbacks.

你們在面臨這麼多的挫折時，有非常棒的態度。

Often on graduation day we look for heroes.

在畢業的日子，我們常常會尋找英雄。

I see them right here among us.

我就在我們之中看到了。

We don't have to look far for inspiration.

我們不需要到遠處尋找啓發了。

We each have the potential to do great things.

我們每個人都有潛力完成偉大的事情。

Celebrate what you have accomplished.

慶祝你所完成的事情。

Look forward to what you have yet to achieve.

期待你尚未達成的事情。

** ————————————

attitude〔'ætə,tjud〕*n.* 態度
in the face of 面對　　setback〔'sɛt,bæk〕*n.* 挫折
look for 尋找　　hero〔'hɪro〕*n.* 英雄
right here 就在這裡　　among〔ə'mʌŋ〕*prep.* 在…之間
inspiration〔,ɪnspə'reʃən〕*n.* 激勵；啓發
potential〔pə'tɛnʃəl〕*n.* 潛力　　celebrate〔'sɛlə,bret〕*v.* 慶祝
accomplish〔ə'kɑmplɪʃ〕*v.* 完成　　***look forward to*** 期待
have yet to V. 尚未～　　achieve〔ə'tʃiv〕*v.* 達成；完成

10

○背景說明

　　開學和畢業，可以說是在學校階段必經的路程。本書第一課，教你如何在開學時介紹自己，最後一課，教你如何在畢業時表達感謝致詞。背完了本課，就可以知道如何在台上侃侃而談，當一位有自信的畢業生代表。

1. *We are all entering a new stage of life*.

enter〔'ɛntɚ〕*v.* 進入　　stage〔stedʒ〕*n.* 階段；舞台

　　這句話的意思是「我們都要進入一個新的人生階段。」stage 原本的意思是「舞台」，引伸為「階段」；英國文豪莎士比亞也曾說：

　　All the world's a *stage*, and all the men and
　　　women merely players.
　　（世界是一個舞台，而男男女女是眾演員。）

　　The product is still at a developmental *stage*.
　　（這產品仍處於研發階段。）

merely〔'mɪrlɪ〕*adv.* 僅僅；只（= *only*）
player〔'pleɚ〕*n.* 演員　　product〔'pradəkt〕*n.* 產品
developmental〔dɪˌvɛləp'mɛntl̩〕*adj.* 發展的；開發的

這句話也可以說成：

　　This is a new beginning for all of us.
　　（這對我們所有人來說都是新的開始。）

10

Today marks the first day of the rest of
our lives.

（今天代表著我們往後生命的開始。）

beginning〔bɪˋgɪnɪŋ〕*n.* 開始
mark〔mɑrk〕*v.* 表示　　rest〔rɛst〕*n.* 剩下；殘餘

2. *This cannot be said for all schools.*

這句話的意思是「並非所有學校都能這麼說。」
所指的是「並非所有的學校狀況都是一樣的。」類似
的說法有：

Although the product is doing pretty well in
the Japanese market, the same *cannot be said
for* foreign markets.

（雖然這個產品在日本的市場表現很好，但在國外的市
場則不是如此。）

Most tourists have a lot of fun in the Philippines
but the same *cannot be said for* people who
want to do business in the country.

（大多數的旅客在菲律賓玩得很愉快，但對想要在那國
家做生意的人來說，則不是如此。）

10

do well 進展好；表現好　　pretty〔ˋprɪtɪ〕*adv.* 相當；非常
Japanese〔͵dʒæpəˋniz〕*adj.* 日本的
market〔ˋmɑrkɪt〕*n.* 市場　　foreign〔ˋfɔrɪn〕*adj.* 外國的
have fun 玩得愉快　　tourist〔ˋturɪst〕*n.* 觀光客
the Philippines 菲律賓群島　　*do business* 做生意
country〔ˋkauntrɪ〕*n.* 國家

這句話也可以說成：

Some schools are better than others.

（有些學校比其他學校好。）

Not all schools are considered equal.

（並非所有學校都被認爲是同樣的。）

consider〔kənˈsɪdə〕v. 認爲
equal〔ˈikwəl〕adj. 同樣的；相等的

3. ***We had our families supporting us along the way.***

family〔ˈfæməlɪ〕n. 家人
support〔səˈport〕v. 支持
along the way 一路上；沿途

　　這句話的意思是「我們一路上有家人支持著我們。」
這裡的 have 不是「使役動詞」，而是「有」的意思，原
句爲：

We had our families who supported us
　　along the way.

　　who 省略後，須將 supported 改成 supporting，變成：
We had our families supporting us...。注意以下 have 作
爲「使役動詞」後面接「原型動詞」（表示主動）和「過去
分詞」（表示被動）的用法：

I'll ***have someone clean*** out your room.

（我會叫人把你的房間打掃乾淨。）

10

I'm *having all the carpets cleaned*.

（我會把所有的地毯弄乾淨。）

另外，如果是 have *sb.* V-ing，也是表示「使某人
（做）」，但是這時候，後面的動作是「開始…」或「持
續…」的意思，強迫意味較弱，例如：

He *had us all laughing* through the meal.

（吃飯時，他讓我們一直笑個不停。）

Within minutes he *had* the whole *audience*
laughing and clapping.

（幾分鐘內，他就讓全場聽眾
開始又笑又拍手。）

through〔θru〕*prep.* 整個（期間、時間）當中
meal〔mil〕*n.* 用餐時間　　within〔wɪðˈɪn〕*prep.* 在…之內
audience〔ˈɔdɪəns〕*n.* 聽眾；觀眾

這句話也可以說成：

Fortunately, our families were always there
for us.

（幸運的是，我們的家人總是準備好要幫助我們。）

However, we had our families there to
support us.

（然而，我們有親人準備好要支持我們。）

fortunately〔ˈfɔrtʃənɪtlɪ〕*adv.* 幸虧；幸運地
however〔hauˈɛvɚ〕*adv.* 然而

4. *The friendships that we have made here will last a lifetime.*

friendship〔'frɛnd,ʃɪp〕*n.* 友誼
last〔læst〕*v.* 持續
lifetime〔'laɪf,taɪm〕*n.* 一生；終生

　　這句話的意思是「我們在這裡建立的友誼將會持續終生。」雖然友誼長存，但是英文也有一句話用來表示事物終會有結束的時候：

　　All good things come to an end.
　　（【諺】天下沒有不散的宴席。）
　　【*come to an end* 結束】

這句話也可以說成：

　　The friends we have made are friends for life.
　　（我們所交的朋友是一輩子的。）

　　We will be friends for the rest of our lives.
　　（我們將終生是朋友。）

　　make friends 交朋友　　*for life* 終生
　　the rest of one's life 餘生

5. *You have had such a great attitude in the face of so many setbacks.*

attitude〔'ætə,tjud〕*n.* 態度　　*in the face of* 面對
setback〔'sɛt,bæk〕*n.* 挫折

10

　　這句話的意思是「你們在面臨這麼多挫折時，有非

常棒的態度。」有句話說：Attitude is everything.
（態度決定一切。）可見態度對於處理危機的重要性。
這句話也可以說成：

> You have faced every challenge with
> courage. （你們都勇敢地面對所有挑戰。）

> You never let anything stand in your way.
> （你們絕不會讓任何事物阻礙你們。）

face〔fes〕*v.* 面對　　challenge〔'tʃælɪndʒ〕*n.* 挑戰
courage〔'kɜɪdʒ〕*n.* 勇氣
with courage 勇敢地（= *courageously*）
stand in *one's* ***way*** 擋住某人的路；阻礙某人

6. *We don't have to look far for inspiration.*
look for 尋找
inspiration〔͵ɪnspə'reʃən〕*n.* 激勵；啓發

　　　這句話的字面意思是「我們不需要看很遠來尋找啓
發。」「不看遠」就是「近在眼前」，所以這句話翻成
「我們不需要到遠處尋找啓發了。」也可以說成：

> Inspiration is all around us.
> （啓發就在我們身邊。）

> We are surrounded by inspiration.
> （我們被啓發所包圍。）

be around *sb.* 在某人身旁
surround〔sə'raund〕*v.* 包圍

10

● 作文範例

A Graduation Speech

Faculty and students, family and friends, it is my honor to be here. To be chosen as the voice of this class is something I will always remember.

Today is a day to be thankful and inspired. We have received a great education thanks to our fine administration and teachers. Whatever we decide to do next, we will benefit from what we have learned here. We can *also* be thankful for our families. They have supported us through three years of ups and downs. *Finally*, we can be thankful for each other. The friendships that we have made here will last a lifetime.

Often on graduation day we look outside for heroes. I see them right here among us. We each have the potential to do great things. When you leave here today, celebrate what you have accomplished and look forward to what you have yet to achieve.

10

○中文翻譯

畢業致詞

各位老師，各位同學，所有家人朋友，很榮幸來到這裡。我將永遠記得，我獲選代表本班發言。

今天是要感謝和受到啟發的日子。我們已經接受了很棒的教育，這都多虧了我們良好的行政當局和老師。無論我們接下來決定要做什麼，我們在這裡的所學都會對我們有益。我們也要感謝我們的家人，他們支持著我們度過三年來的起伏。最後，我們也要感謝彼此，我們在這裡建立的友誼將會持續終生。

在畢業的日子，我們常常向外尋找英雄，我就在我們之中找到了。我們彼此都有潛力完成偉大的事情。當你今天離開這裡，要慶祝你所完成的事物，並期待你尚未達成的。

10

這10篇演講稿，
你都背下來了嗎？
現在請利用下面的提示，
不斷地複習。

以下你可以看到每篇演講稿的格式，
三句為一組，九句為一段，每篇演講稿共
三段，27句，看起來是不是輕鬆好背呢？
不要猶豫，趕快開始背了！每篇
演講稿只要能背到1分半鐘內，
就終生不忘！

1. Self-Introduction

Hello, my name is Donald.
I am a new student at this school.
It is my pleasure to be here.

This is an exciting time.
There are many new faces.
There will be many new names to learn.

I hope to meet all of you.
I hope to be your friend.
Let me tell you about myself.

I like reading and playing violin.
I speak three languages.
I would like to speak good English ....

I come from a small family.
I don't have any siblings.
Therefore, I'm very close to my parents.

I have big plans for the future.
I would like to study medicine.
I want to be a doctor.

Of course, I am here to learn.
But I also want to make friends.
Maybe we can have fun at the ....

Here's what you can expect from me.
I am very polite and respectful.
I am always willing to help.

The next few years will be interesting.
We will share many experiences.
I wish the best for each and every ....

2. My Parents

My parents play a big part in my life.
They have molded my character.
They have been my role models.

My parents have good moral character.
They don't smoke, drink, or gamble.
They are patient and good listeners.

My parents demonstrate good virtue ....
They teach me to have respect.
They teach me to be kind to others.

My parents have raised three children.
All of us are well-adjusted.
Their influence is the reason.

My parents believe in strong ....
They take time to listen to us.
They understand our problems.

One time, my sister failed a test.
My parents did not scold or judge her.
They simply encouraged her to try ....

Having patience is important for ....
My parents always go the extra mile.
Their patience has no limit.

Being a parent is a tough job.
It comes with a lot of responsibility.
Sacrifices must be made.

In modern times, parenting is ....
It takes good character to raise ....
That's why my parents make me ....

3. My Mentor

A mentor does not offer wisdom.
A mentor inspires questions.
A mentor should help you help ....

My mentor is Ms. Chen.
She is a teacher at my school.
I have been her student for three years.

She is a great teacher.
She teaches us things we can use ....
She also teaches us things we can ....

When I was younger, I wanted to ....
But now, I want to be a journalist.
It's all because of Ms. Chen.

No one has influenced me more ....
It was in her class that I learned to ....
Now it's my passion.

Ms. Chen convinced me to enter a ....
She helped me edit the story.
She was there with me every step ....

Then Ms. Chen told me I had won!
I had a special reason for being happy.
I knew she was proud of my ....

Ms. Chen is very kind.
She is always ready to help.
She gives advice and encouragement.

Some day I will be a great writer.
Some day I will not be Ms. Chen's ....
But she will always be my mentor.

4. My Idol

Some of my friends idolize pop stars.
Others worship professional athletes.
However, my idol is much closer ....

I have always looked up to my ....
I have admired him for all his success.
Uncle Mike is my idol.

He is the only person in my family ....
He has shown me that anyone can ....
His success has given me hope that ....

Uncle Mike has inspired me to ....
He encourages me to aim higher ....
He never lets me take the easy ....

Uncle Mike's success amazes me.
It baffles me how he did it.
Only a special person can do what ....

Our family was never rich.
Everybody worked very hard.
Nothing was ever given to us.

Uncle Mike created his company ....
It took him ten years, but it finally ....
He sold it for two hundred million ...!

Uncle Mike set an example.
With determination, I can ....
Nothing can stop me.

Uncle Mike has always believed in me.
He has supported everything I do.
He gives me the inspiration I need.

5. My Buddy

It is very hard to find a true and ….
I am very lucky that I have a good ….
His name is James.

James is very friendly.
He is also is a good person.
He has all the qualities we seek in ….

James is a very helpful person.
For instance, he helps his parents ….
He mows the lawn and cleans the ….

James is hardworking and punctual.
He likes doing his work on time.
For example, his homework is ….

James always attends his classes.
He is always prepared for his tests.
He works part-time to have pocket ….

Finally, James is very honest.
He speaks the truth and hates lying.
When he makes a mistake, he ….

Having a buddy like James is ….
He is a good person to be around.
He helps me stay on track.

We do things outside of school, too.
Sometimes we play sports.
Sometimes we go to the movies.

In conclusion, James is a great buddy.
He makes everyone very comfortable.
He will never let you down.

6. My Happiest Moment

Every life has its ups and downs.
Sorrow and joy are two parts of life.
In fact, life is full of good and bad.

Some things are forgotten.
Others leave a lasting impression.
We will never forget them.

Such a moment came to me last year.
I received a perfect score on my ….
It was the happiest moment of my life.

Before the exams, I was very nervous.
When I learned the result, I was so ….
I felt like I had won the whole world.

To celebrate, my friends and I went ….
The picnic spot was crowded.
We enjoyed our snacks.

We danced and sang songs.
But there was a loud cry from the lake.
A small boy was drowning in the …!

Fortunately, I am a good swimmer.
Immediately, I jumped into the lake.
After a great struggle, I pulled the ….

The boy was in bad shape but alive.
We were all overjoyed.
Saving his life was awesome.

This event taught me a lesson.
I realized how precious life is.
That was my happiest moment.

7. My Favorite Movie

Movies come in many different ....
Watching movies is entertaining.
I personally enjoy watching ....

Most of the time, I like to watch ....
I also prefer movies that teach a lesson.
My favorite movie is Save the Last ....

It has romance, music and dance.
I was impressed by Julia Stiles, ...
She is my favorite actress.

Save the Last Dance is set in New ....
It's about a girl who wants to be a ....
Then her mother suddenly dies.

Sarah has to go live with her dad.
She also transfers to a new school.
She has no friends until she meets ....

Chenille helps Sarah and shows her ....
She gets to know Chenille's brother, ...
She later falls in love with him.

Derrick teaches her how to dance ....
At last, Sarah makes it into Julliard.
She finally achieves her dream.

It's my favorite movie because I ....
I was surprised how quickly Sarah ....
It inspired me to give it a try.

The lesson of the movie is to be ....
Sometimes life is a struggle.
You must always work hard and ....

8. My Favorite Subject

Some students prefer to study math.
Others prefer to study history.
It's easier to memorize things ....

My favorite subject is English.
Others have tried to discourage me.
They say I am wasting my time.

Some people think English is useless.
However, I think it's interesting ....
I love learning different languages.

I especially enjoy reading English ....
Reading in itself is a great pleasure.
English has a wealth of literature.

It gives us an insight into human ....
We realize what actions bring what ....
We learn to look for deeper meaning.

In addition to reading, I like to ....
I have several foreign friends.
We have language exchanges.

English is the international language.
It is an open door to the world.
English can take you places.

Learning English will help me in ....
I plan to study overseas.
English is a necessity.

Studying and practicing English is ....
Every day is a new set of challenges.
That is why English is my favorite ....

9. My Dream

I am a lucky person.
I am lucky because I know what ....
I have always had a direction in life.

I have many hopes and ambitions ....
However, there is one thing I want ....
I want to be a buyer for a clothing ....

I have been interested in fashion ....
I love to go shopping for clothes.
I read all the fashion magazines.

So far, I have taken steps toward ....
My formal education is the starting ....
I believe that it will continue to be ....

My first and foremost plan is to ....
I consider this to be a huge ....
After graduation, I will go to college.

In college, I will study business ....
I will dedicate myself to realizing ....
I will obtain the knowledge I need.

What happens after that is hard to ....
My education will be my foundation.
However, the world changes so ....

I must remain flexible.
As I get older, I will see things ....
Perhaps my dream will change.

The most important thing is to stay ....
Now I work toward making it real.
I will succeed in anything I choose ....

10. A Graduation Speech

Faculty and students.
Family and friends.
It is my honor to be here.

Today is a day to be thankful.
Today is a day to be inspired.
We are all entering a new stage of life.

We have received a great education.
We are prepared to face challenges.
We have been given a priceless gift.

This cannot be said for all schools.
Here we have had a high degree of ....
Whatever you decide to do next, ...

We can also be thankful for our ....
These past three years included ....
We had our families supporting us ....

Finally, we can be thankful for ....
The friendships that we have made ....
I hope we will continue to be there ....

Now, what can we be inspired by ...?
I am inspired by you—my ....
You have had such a great attitude ....

Often on graduation day we look ....
I see them right here among us.
We don't have to look far for ....

We each have the potential to do ....
Celebrate what you have ....
Look forward to what you have yet ....

本書所有人

姓名 ＿＿＿＿＿＿＿＿＿＿＿＿＿＿＿＿ 電話 ＿＿＿＿＿＿＿＿＿＿＿＿＿＿

地址 ＿＿＿＿＿＿＿＿＿＿＿＿＿＿＿＿＿＿＿＿＿＿＿＿＿＿＿＿＿＿＿＿＿

（如拾獲本書，請通知本人領取，感激不盡。）

「小學生英語演講」背誦記錄表

篇　　　　　　　　名	口試通過日期	口試老師簽名
1. Self-Introduction	年　　月　　日	
2. My Parents	年　　月　　日	
3. My Mentor	年　　月　　日	
4. My Idol	年　　月　　日	
5. My Buddy	年　　月　　日	
6. My Happiest Moment	年　　月　　日	
7. My Favorite Movie	年　　月　　日	
8. My Favorite Subject	年　　月　　日	
9. My Dream	年　　月　　日	
10. A Graduation Speech	年　　月　　日	
全部 10 篇演講總複試	年　　月　　日	

　　自己背演講，很難專心，背給別人聽，是最有效的方法。練習的程序是：自己背 ➡ 背給同學聽 ➡ 背給老師聽 ➡ 在全班面前發表演講。可在教室裡、任何表演舞台或台階上，二、三個同學一組練習，比賽看誰背得好，效果甚佳。

　　天天聽著 CD，模仿美國人的發音和語調，英文自然就越說越溜。英語演講背多後，隨時都可以滔滔不絕，口若懸河。